Helena O'Connor lives in sunny Australia, where she can write with coffee, treats, and a nice view of the sea. Having previously worked in neuroscience research and clinical psychology, she now writes full time across fantasy, science fiction, and horror. Her work tends towards bittersweet themes and dark dystopias, more often than not with a wry sense of humour.

Her short fiction has appeared in anthologies such as *Killer Creatures Down Under: Horror Stories with Bite* (IFWG publishing) and *It Was All a Dream: An Anthology of Bad Horror Tropes Done Right* (Hungry Shadow Press), as well as literary magazines such as *Nature: Futures, Aurealis, Andromeda Spaceways Magazine, Abyss & Apex,* and *Kaleidotrope*.

Helena is an avid video game player and drinker of coffee. You can find her on socials @HelenaFiction where she posts about games, the writing life, and cute cats.

Willow Close

by
Helena O'Connor

Willow Close

ISBN-13: 978-1-923382-13-8

Printed in Palatino Linotype and Caudex.

IFWG Publishing International
Gold Coast

www.ifwgpublishing.com

Acknowledgements

Willow Close will always have a special place in my heart. I have published several short stories, but this is my very first book. It was several years in the making and there are many people without whom it would not have been possible. I am incredibly grateful to everyone involved.

A huge thank you to my wonderful publisher Gerry Huntman and IFWG publishing, for your wisdom, support, and guidance throughout the process, to my editor Noel Osualdini and proofreader Stephen McCracken, for their unfailing attention to detail, and to artist Greg Chapman, for creating such a stunning cover. I appreciate you all so much.

Thank you to my family and friends, for reading drafts, listening to me talk about my weird and wonderful worlds, and for always encouraging my dreams.

And a special thanks to you, the readers, for taking this journey. I hope you enjoy my words.

Prologue

Kess was in the dark place again. Surrounded by a strange forest with tall, twisted trees. Blackened soot-smoke branches swayed softly to the tune of some unspoken wind. The space pressed like a blanket. Whispers, dark and foreboding, soft edges filled with evil intent, dripped malice into every particle of air in the dark place. It was suffocating, desperate, saturated with demonic desires. A closed-in, locked up agony. It was her only sanctuary.

Kess huddled among the tall trees and listened to the whisper-wind. The balm of the breeze soothed her open wounds. She hated the dark place. But there were places she hated more. This at least was familiar, and safe in its own way. The dark place had never hurt her. And it wouldn't hurt her, as long as she did what it said.

In the cool, damp mist, Kess drew her knees to her chest and waited. The darkness pressed in, spreading over her senses, numb and chilling. A trickle of light fell between the ring of tall trees, patchy and weak, eroded by the thick dark. Into this filtered light stepped a small, dappled deer. The deer sniffed the edges of the trees. Its limbs were like twigs, the skin paper thin. So delicate. So pure.

Kess held her breath. The fawn sniffed its way to where she sat waiting. Carefully, she stretched out her fingers. The deer licked at her hand. All was quiet in the dark place. The whispers had stopped. The brooding dark hovered, watching.

With a sharp, practiced movement, Kess lunged. She gathered the deer to her chest, its tiny limbs pressed tight against her. It struggled, but its feeble efforts were no match for her strength. Resigned, it leaned into her, limbs shaking. Kess lowered her mouth to kiss the deer's head. She drank in its animal smell. This time she would win.

The trees rustled with passing messages. A dull thud echoed in the distance. A crashing, breaking sound. Trees and branches snapped, falling to the muffled ground. He was awake and coming towards them, fast. The hunter. She could not bear to see him again. Kess cradled the tiny deer in her arms. She took a deep breath and squeezed her eyes shut. It was time to run.

With her eyes firmly closed, Kess rose. She held the deer to her chest. Sniffing the air, she spun on the spot, marking her direction. Her ears caught the forest sounds and told her which way to run. The crash of the hunter echoed behind her. Kess tightened her whole body, readying herself. Then she sprang from the clearing and sprinted into the forest.

All at once, the trees had knives. Even with her eyes closed, she could sense the glints of silver, the daggers sharp and furious, all around her. The deer's fragile heart beat against her own, faster and faster. A tiny, hummingbird flutter.

The path was memorized. She had been here, so many times before. There had been so many losses. She closed her mind. She had to concentrate, could not let herself think of what happened every time she failed. The crunch of brittle bones. The blood that soaked her nightshirt. The bleat and cry of life ebbing away from the small, warm body cradled in her arms.

The forest never hurt her. It only wanted the deer. Yet the voices rang in her ears as she ran. The twisted trees, with their whispers, louder and louder:

Save the fawn! Save the fawn! Save the fawn!

She was getting close. She could almost feel the way out. A glimmering light showed red against her eyelids, flicking through the shadows of the trees. The light marked the way out of the dark place. All she had to do was reach it. Kess hurtled through the dark. Faster and faster. Legs burning, lungs aching. She had to reach the light. Had to save the fawn.

The light burned brighter against her eyelids. She was closer than she had ever been. Soon she would have to open her eyes, to see what lay in front of her.

Kess stumbled from the forest and opened her eyes. A portal, green and swirling, lay directly in front of her. The deer bleated, warm and small and precious. She was going to save the fawn. This time.

Kess leaped towards the portal. As she stretched towards the light, deer clasped to her chest, a noose tightened around her neck. She was hauled backwards. The hunter had her. Ravenous claws grabbed at her nightshirt, pulling her back into the forest. With the last bit of her strength, Kess threw the deer towards the light.

The deer gave a bleat of surprise, but it landed on its tiny legs and lunged towards the portal. It bounded like a gazelle.

Kess thudded abruptly to a stop, lying in the mud and dirt. The pressure dragging her backwards into the forest was gone. A dark shape flashed across her vision.

The deer gathered itself to leap through the portal. It took a final delicate step and then it was airborne, sailing towards freedom and light.

With a crash like thunder, a surge of pain that echoed deep in Kess's bones, a dark shape collided with the deer, knocking it from its trajectory. A form made of shadow and smoke. The hunter. Jaws, deep and ravenous, closed around the deer's throat and bit down with a sickening crunch. The deer's limbs fluttered, like tiny butterflies in the night. Another crunch and the flutters stopped. The deer hung lifeless, blood spilling to the ground.

The hunter was a man-monster. Too vast to be human, not animal enough to be anything else. Spines erupting from flesh, and misshapen growths along visible skin. Limbs thick as trees. A predator with a human face.

Blood dripped from the deer. The hunter smiled around his prey. He looked Kess in the eyes. Saw her fluttering heart. Kess opened her mouth to scream, but there was no sound. The dark place had eaten her words. Her thoughts. She struggled to remember where she was, who she was. The hunter's smile stretched too wide, the smell of blood choked the air, the deer dangled lifeless and spent, as the world lurched and spun.

A vast light opened above, sucking her away from the dark place…

Kess opened her eyes in the dark of a bedroom. In the light from the window, she could just make out something hovering in the dark. A long tentacle seemed to reach out from the wall, a writhing, squirming tendril hanging just above her head. She could see suckers, little mouths, opening and closing. Kess couldn't find the breath to scream. She felt suffocated, like she was drowning.

The light flicked on in the small bedroom. Kess blinked, staring into space. There was no tentacle. There was nothing above her, just the matte white of the ceiling. A woman hurried in. Was she Kess's Mother? She looked familiar but something didn't feel right. Kess didn't have a mother, did she?

The woman bent down and felt Kess's forehead. "Another nightmare?"

Kess nodded, trying to rearrange the blankets from where they were balled at the end of the bed. Her heart was fluttering with panic and disorientation, but the woman seemed to mean no harm. It even felt reassuring, after the dark place, to have a motherly presence fussing over her.

The woman remade the bed with trembling hands. "You're having more bad dreams, lately. Is anything wrong at school? With your friends?"

Kess shook her head. She reached to smooth out her long hair, expecting it to be balled up like her sheets had been in a big, frizzy mess, but instead it was cut short and ragged. Strange. She ran her fingers through the space where her hair usually was. The mother-lady sat on the edge of the bed, tight brown curls bobbing as she wrung her hands. Kess could smell her perfume, soft like lilac blossoms. From somewhere else in the house, the living room presumably, came the low buzz of the television.

"Honey." The woman's forehead creased. "I haven't told your father yet, but your principal, Mr Davies, called me. A few days ago."

Kess let her eyes roam the room. Her small single bed was made with blue striped sheets. A flimsy-looking, brown wooden cupboard sat across from her, door firmly closed. A work desk sat against the other wall, with one of those flexible-stand lamps. She could see a schoolbag sitting on the chair, a bright Transformers pattern on the side. Optimus Prime was giving her the thumbs up. Cool, but didn't her schoolbag usually have pink butterflies? The bag was half open, a load of schoolbooks poking out. Papers lay strewn across the desk. It looked as though she hadn't finished her maths homework. She wondered if she would get in trouble.

Light spilled into the bedroom from a single window. Along the windowsill sat a row of dead, wingless flies. Gross. How had *they* gotten there? Why? She couldn't remember. A mass of memories pressed against the back of her mind. School, friends, a life that wasn't hers. The room was both familiar, and not. In the eerie half-light, it seemed strange and other. But it was also where she belonged. Here, with her mother. The dream flitted across her mind. The deer. The hunter. The dark place. She belonged there too.

Mother frowned. "Mr Davies said you've been drawing pictures in class. Apparently, they're a bit…disturbing."

Kess's eyes roamed upwards to the corner of the room above the desk. The place where, a moment before, a writhing tentacle had been reaching. A crack in the plaster loomed in the wall, running down from the corner where it joined with the ceiling. In the memory that wasn't hers, the crack had been there forever. It had always been. She tried to compare the memory to the crack in front of her. She could have sworn this crack was wider, that its branching tendrils had extended farther down the wall since last she'd looked. When had she last looked? As she peered, a light seemed to flicker in the crack. Shapes moved within. A shudder crept down her spine.

"Are you listening to me?" The sharpness in Mother's voice drew her attention back. She got the feeling she had missed a chunk of the conversation. There was something hypnotic about the crack. As if she could lose time, just staring into it.

Her mother's eyes were wide, worried. "He said the other students have been picking on you. That you've been getting into fights. Is that true?"

"I don't know." The voice was raspy and strange in her throat, deeper than it should have been. Not her voice. Her heart pounded. As she cleared her throat, she could see the homework and the schoolbag. None of it was hers. Or was it? She searched her mind. She couldn't remember school, her friends. Had people been picking on her? Suddenly, she didn't know. Panic raced in her veins. Her eyes drifted back to the crack in the wall. A dark, black substance was seeping out. It looked like oil. It dripped down the wall, onto the thin, grey carpet.

"I don't want to tell your father, but you can't go getting into fights. The principal said your grades are slipping and that you aren't doing your homework." Mother's eyes flittered, like nervous bugs, around the room. They landed on the desk. "Those papers—is that your homework?"

"I don't think it's finished yet," said Kess with her new raspy voice, eyes fixed on the wall. Dark shapes moved in the light behind the crack. Oil poured forth, flowing down the wall to the carpet. A blackish patch was forming where it soaked the fabric.

"Honey... What are you looking at?" Her mother finally turned to look at the wall. She stood up and strode over to where the oil was trickling down the faded paintwork. "What on earth is that?"

"Don't touch it!" Kess swung her legs out of bed in a hurry, fear shooting through her stomach. Her feet brushed the carpet and she recoiled. Had she somehow grown taller overnight?

Mother had already stretched out a finger and smeared it through the oil on the wall. She moved into the light, staring. Rubbing the oil between her fingers.

"Wash it off!" Kess said urgently.

Mother ignored her. "It must be some sort of leak. But it looks like engine oil." She stuck her head out into the corridor. "Bill? Come look at this."

A rustling came from the living room. There was a click as the TV was switched off and in the sudden absence of sound the dull thud of footsteps echoed along the corridor.

Mother looked at Kess nervously. "I won't tell him about the fights, or the homework. Not tonight. But you must try harder. Promise me?"

Kess nodded. She didn't want to get in trouble with Father. The memories in the back of her mind knew that would be very bad.

"What is it?" A man appeared at the door, looked vaguely annoyed. His greying hair stood up in a tangled patch at the back where it had been crushed against the velvet of his old recliner chair.

"Bill, look at the wall here. It looks like some kind of oil."

"Don't touch it!" said Kess again, as insistent as she dared. The oil was seeping fast now, in a rivulet thick like honey. It shone with oil slick colors in the light, viscous and vicious.

Father ignored her. "That is strange." He ran a finger through the oil and rubbed it between his fingers. With a grunt, he traced its track from ceiling to floor. He clicked his tongue against his teeth as he bent to the floor, pulling at the carpet, examining the stain. Then he straightened up, staring balefully at the slick on the wall.

Finally, he spun with a glare, dead grey eyes boring into her. "What have you been doing in here?"

"Nothing." Kess's heart leaped into her throat. She hadn't been doing anything. She had never even been here. How could she explain to these people?

Mother put a calming hand on his arm. "Bill. It's some sort of leak, don't you think?"

Her father harrumphed and tapped his foot. "Expensive. To pull up this carpet, to fix the plaster." The roll of flesh at his neck, visible under the collar of his plaid work shirt, was slowly turning red. "Very expensive." A blue vein throbbed in his forehead.

"Wasn't there something on the news," her voice shook, "about trouble over at the old chemical plant? You don't think…"

"I'll call Lionel." He frowned at Kess for a moment longer, then turned on his heel and left the room. His footsteps thumped along the corridor to the phone. They could hear him spinning the dial, with a lot more force than necessary.

"I'll make him something extra nice for dinner tomorrow." Mother wrung her hands. "And we won't say anything about the principal. Just do your homework and try not to get in any more trouble at school. Please?" Her voice trembled, and Kess nodded.

Father's raised voice echoed down the corridor. Suddenly he was yelling. "What do you mean, a spill? Who's going to pay for that?" The thin walls shook. From another room, there was a gurgle and cry. Then a baby started wailing in earnest.

Mother sighed. "He woke Mikey." She leaned over and kissed Kess's head. "Try to go back to sleep, honey. We'll sort all this out in the morning." She fluttered out of the room, switching the light off as she went. Kess lay back down in bed. Father was still yelling at someone on the other end of the phone. In her parents' bedroom, her baby brother was squealing.

There was a crash as Father slammed down the phone. She could hear him stomping back to the living room. After a moment, the television flicked on. The low thrum of music and voices filled the house. Mikey gave another, plaintive wail.

"Shut him up, Gayle, or I swear…"

"It's fine, he's fine." Mother called from the bedroom. Mikey gurgled a few times, then settled. Kess felt a rush of protectiveness. Whenever Father was angry, she worried about poor, defenseless Mikey. Funny. She couldn't remember his birth. He was just…*here*. Like her. But she knew it was her job to protect him.

Kess closed her eyes tight and tried to sleep. She tried to ignore the branching crack and the oil that seemed to bleed from somewhere deep within. Everything was all wrong. If she could just get through the night, without any more dreams of the dark place. Surely, when she woke, she would be back in her own room, her own life…

The dilapidated, old house at 149 Willow Close shuddered in the night air. On its roof, a thick patch of oil oozed and seeped through the cracks.

K ess trudged slowly home, muddy backpack slung over her shoulder. The Transformers patch had been half torn away. Father would be angry. A huge purple bruise was already spreading around her left eye. There was no getting around the situation. It was clear she'd been fighting, but she couldn't remember the details. Couldn't remember the school day, or the bus ride home. She had been trying to sleep in a room that wasn't hers, then all of a sudden, she was walking home to the house that she'd never lived in. Her knuckles were bloody as she grasped the creaky old gate and pushed it open.

She walked across the uneven paving to the door. The house, whitewashed and ragged, sagged on its small plot. Weeds grew in the garden, and the grass was uneven. She had been supposed to mow the lawn and poison the weeds. More trouble. A newspaper lay on the patio. Strange. Mother usually brought it in as soon as it was delivered. Father liked to read the paper with his morning coffee. Kess picked up the paper, pulled out her house key and went to let herself in. But the door was already ajar.

She pushed into the house, door creaking wide, and stood in the entrance. All was quiet. Kess pushed the door closed behind her and dropped her bag under the coat hooks. It came to rest against Father's work boots. He must be home already. A half day perhaps.

The corridor stretched out in front of her. As she watched, it seemed to telescope outwards, growing and growing, until her head spun.

The bungalow split itself off the corridor into the two bedrooms and living room, with the kitchen right at the end. The kitchen door led out to a small garden with a work shed at the back. Father might be out there but where was Mother? She usually rushed into the corridor when she heard the front door. Perhaps she was taking a nap with Mikey. Unlikely, if Father was already home, though.

The house was silent without the blare of the television. She could hear birds calling outside, the whisper of the wind through the trees down the street. And a soft *snick, snick, snick*, that seemed to be coming from somewhere inside the house.

Kess walked slowly down the corridor. She pushed open the door to her parents' bedroom. Clothes lay draped across the bed and floor. A half-full suitcase was propped against the wall. It looked as if someone had tried to pack in a hurry and been interrupted. The house was usually neat as a pin. The strewn clothes were out of place. What was happening? There were red smears on the walls that looked like blood. No sign of her parents.

"Mom?" called Kess, hesitantly. There was no answer.

She stepped back into the corridor, heart thumping, and opened the door to her own room. Everything was as it should be, except for the oil that oozed down the wall and made a puddle in the carpet. The stain was a lot larger than it had been last night. Had she checked it this morning before she left? She couldn't remember.

"Mom?" she called again, louder. Still no answer. The rattle of a saucepan was coming from the kitchen. She hurried down the corridor. There was no one in the kitchen. Only a cutting board with sliced onions and peppers, and small pieces of pale sausage. A pot of potatoes was bubbling away on the stove, the lid clattering. Kess crossed the floor, lifted the lid, and peered into the pot. Potato steam coursed into the air. The original waterline was far above where the last remains of the water now hissed and steamed. The potatoes in the pot were mangled and discolored. With a frown, Kess turned off the gas. The pot had almost boiled dry. Even she knew that was dangerous.

Kess stood in the kitchen, listening. Without the rattle of the pot, she could hear better. The *snick, snick, snick* was coming from the bathroom.

As she turned to leave the kitchen, the cutting board caught her eye. The onions were the wrong color. They were red, as if stained by the peppers. Kess took a closer look at the small pieces of sausage. Her heart stuttered. They looked like fingers. She picked one up. A brightly painted fingernail stared back at her. It was the same color as her mother's fingernails. Blood oozed and dripped from the mangled end of the finger. Kess dropped it and backed away, hands clutched to her mouth. The cutting board was soaked in blood.

"Mom!!" Kess yelled from between her hands. The finger rolled off the bench and hit the kitchen floor with a squishy thud.

Kess ran to the bathroom door. Heart in her throat, she knocked on the door. "Mom?" There was no sound, except the gentle *snick, snick, snick*, which was definitely coming from behind the door. She tapped again, louder, banging on the door. "Mom!"

Biting the inside of her cheek, Kess gave the door a shove. She had expected it to be locked, but it swung open. Mother was hunched over on the tiles, leaning against the bath. Water dripped from the taps. A grimy soap ring was visible around the edge of the bath. Patches of crimson spread out across the pale, blue tiles.

As Kess watched, Mother drew the large kitchen knife, back and forth, across her thighs. *Snick, snick, snick.* Her wrists had deep gashes, slashes of bright red. Blood coursed from the wounds, running across her pale flesh. The blood had stained large patches of her pretty yellow summer dress a deep, dark crimson. Half her fingers were missing. There were cuts on her forehead, glossy red under the fluorescent light, from which blood trickled and ran down her face. Her eyes were blank and lifeless. Her tight, brown curls bobbed as she cut herself.

Kess lunged across the floor, slipping on blood, and knelt beside the woman. Mother's hands were cold and limp, and it was easy to pry the knife away. The blade clattered across the floor. Shaking, Kess wrapped all the bathroom towels around Mother's wounds.

"Why…" Kess's voice shook. "Why…" She didn't know what to say, how to finish the question. Mother's eyes were glazed, unseeing. She rocked back and forth, seemingly unaware of Kess's presence.

With an effort of will, Kess pushed herself to her feet and ran into the corridor. She picked up the phone. With trembling fingers, she rang for an ambulance. The dial was clunky and wouldn't turn. The blood on her hands made everything too slippery. Finally, the call connected. In a trembling voice, Kess tried to explain. The disembodied voice on the other end took her address, told her to keep the patient warm, and rang off. Kess replaced the handset in a daze. Nothing felt real. There was blood smeared all over the phone. She had blood all over her hands and knees. So much blood.

The phone was at the entrance to the kitchen. From here, Kess could see out between the gingham curtains of the small, kitchen window, across the back yard. There was a light on in the garden shed. Father? Her heart leaped at the possibility that she wasn't alone.

Kess raced outside, the flimsy door from the kitchen slapping behind her. She raced across the lawn to the shed, yelling for Father the whole way. There was no answer. The whine of a drill echoed from the shed. He must be so busy working on his project he hadn't even noticed what was happening with Mother. A surge of anger rippled through her.

She tugged open the door to the shed and peered inside, blinking against the gloom. Father stood in the middle of the shed, his face blank. His fingers grasped an electric drill, pressing it hard against his temple. He was squeezing the trigger. The drill whined as it burrowed into his skull. Blood dripped down the side of his face, along with pieces of skull and grey matter. There was a trail of gore down his shirt and trousers, pooling like an oil stain at his feet. The drill whined and whined, digging out pieces of Father's brain.

Kess backed away, out of the shed, hands over her mouth. A wave of nausea caught her, and her knees buckled. She didn't know what to do. Her head spun and squirmed. What was happening? Why would her parents do this? Why would they hurt themselves like this? Blood flashed across her vision and nausea roiled in her stomach. What should she do?

A single thought knocked her remaining breath away. A punch landing right in her gut. Where was baby Mikey? He hadn't been in the house. Where was he? She couldn't hear him, why wasn't he crying? Her eyes roamed the garden. There was a toy sandpit, with a bucket and spade, where Mikey usually played with Mother. He was too small to play by himself. He could barely crawl. She crossed to the sandpit and looked down.

There were ribbons of blood in the sand. A thin trail of blood led away into the bushes. With gut wrenching certainty, Kess knew what she would find if she followed the trail. "No," she murmured, "not Mikey." The world spiraled outwards, like she was being sucked away from reality. Like she was losing her mind.

Kess fell to her knees in the garden. A scream burst from her—a scream of despair issuing from a deep, dark place. A guttural howl of fury, anguish…and vengeance. In the distance, sirens wailed and wailed.

1

The photographs in Mrs Henderson's house were gathering dust. Kestrel Hawkins, Kess for short, ran a finger along the mantlepiece in front of the silver-edged frames. Alternating with the photographs, her own grey-green eyes reflected in the dull glass. She looked pale and drawn. The dreams had been haunting her, night after night. She had barely slept for weeks.

Kess forced a smile, trying to pry open her heavy eyelids. "Are these your kids?"

"Yes, dear." Mrs Henderson placed a tray of homemade lemonade carefully on the glass-top coffee table. "All grown up now, of course." She put a hand to her back, drawing a sharp breath as she slowly straightened up. With a sigh, she pushed her wire-rimmed glasses back onto her nose. "Time passes so quickly."

Kess nodded absently, staring into the frame where two children were laughing together on a colorful swing set. In the foreground, a much younger Mrs Henderson and a jovial-looking man, Mr Henderson presumably, were smiling encouragement. The photo looked as if it had been taken in the back yard of this very house. A tray of lemonade sat on the white, wrought-iron framed patio table. The day was bright and sunny. She could almost smell the crispness in the air.

Ice clinked in the lemonade jug in the living room. The vibrant floral pattern on the tumblers in the photo was similar to the faded motifs on the tumblers Mrs Henderson had just set down.

"How about you, dear?" Mrs Henderson's voice was as warm and sunny as the photo.

"Me?"

"Any children of your own?"

Kess must have made a face, though she hadn't meant to, because Mrs Henderson waved her hands apologetically. "I'm sorry. None of my business." She shuffled around the table, dusting haphazardly at the chairs with a dish towel. "Won't you sit down and have some lemonade? Sorry, there's cat fur just everywhere. I hope you don't mind." She gestured under the dining table. "The big fellow is a shedder."

The dispenser of said fur, an enormous grey cat with long tufted ears and fierce golden eyes, was glowering from under the dining table. Swishing his fluffy tail intently, it looked as though he was pondering why such a strange interloper was here, being offered lemonade. Under his piercing gaze, Kess couldn't help straightening her ponytail. She always wore her hair up when working, in an attempt to look more professional. This morning she had tried to disguise the bright blue streaks running the length of her hair's dark bulk under an elastic topped with a large, blue ribbon. But the cat seemed pretty judgmental about the situation, nonetheless.

"His name is Finnegan," said Mrs Henderson. "Felix, Fiona, and Felicity are out in the yard."

Kess blinked. That was a lot of cats. No wonder there was so much fur. She circled the table, retrieved a glass of lemonade, and squatted obediently on the edge of one of the old, cream-colored leather lounge chairs. The furniture had seen better days, or perhaps Finnegan was as efficient a destroyer of leather as he was an interrogator of visitors. The cracks in the leather could be scratches, or merely old age, difficult to tell. In any case, it seemed the sofa was decaying under the combined attentions of Finnegan, Fiona, Felix and Felicity. It was simultaneously clear that Mrs Henderson had filled her empty nest to the brim with felines. Kess took a sip of lemonade. The bitter acid leapt down her throat and she half-choked.

"Sorry dear, too strong?"

"Not at all." Kess's tastebuds burned with the tartness. She wrangled herself under control and took another delicate sip. "I don't have any," she said to cover the awkwardness as she involuntarily grimaced. Mrs Henderson's lemonade might do better as a scouring agent than a beverage. "Kids, I mean."

"Oh well. Plenty of time. And you've got a good solid frame on you. These girls today, so skinny…"

Kess scratched her hair. She was not what you'd call petite, but not particularly fat either. Not that it mattered. These days, unless you were a starving waif you were deemed overweight by society. Which seemed highly problematic. Kess had decided long ago it was best to just do her own thing.

"Husband?" Mrs Henderson's milk-blue eyes drifted to her ring-free fingers.

"Nope."

"Still living with your parents?"

"They're dead." Kess checked herself. Why had she blurted that out? She took a calming breath. "I was in care, but I don't live with my foster family anymore."

Why did she always feel caught off guard when people asked if she were married or had kids? She had very little interest in life partners or offspring. Perhaps that made her feel defensive in such conversations. She was trying to work on her bluntness, but it came back whenever she felt wrong-footed. Mrs Henderson looked as though she didn't know what to say.

"I'm sorry," Kess said hastily. "What I meant to say is, I live alone." She wouldn't usually admit this, for security reasons, but Mrs Henderson and her cats seemed pretty harmless.

"At least you don't have to worry about the Family Man." Mrs Henderson put her hands to her mouth. "I'm sorry, that's tactless isn't it? I'm out of practice at having company over, you see." She took a couple of huge mouthfuls of lemonade. Apparently, Mrs Henderson was completely immune to the acidic side-effects of the drink, and just as blunt at communication as Kess. That was a relief.

"The Family Man?" Kess asked, distracted by Finnegan who had squeezed out of his hiding place and approached to sniff cautiously at her shoes. She reached out a hand to pat his fuzzy back, but he flipped his elongated ears back. She hesitated. "There's a good kitty."

"Do you not watch the news, dear?"

"Not really." She held her fingers out gently for Finnegan to sniff.

"You young things," said Mrs Henderson. It was a stretch these days, thought Kess, being referred to as young. Mid-30s and counting. An age where other people simply couldn't help themselves—always asking about husbands and kids. She didn't even have a significant other. Not a human one, anyway.

"I have a cat." Kess stretched her hand, slowly, towards Finnegan's fur and he allowed it. Carefully, she stroked his back. A rumbling purr emanated from deep within his steel-grey chest. "So, I guess I don't live alone, not entirely." The purr reverberated around the living room.

"There now, friends at last." Mrs Henderson said happily. "He can probably sense you're a *cat person*. You know, Finnegan, this young lady has helped me a lot this morning. Honestly, I don't know where I'd be."

"It should be just about finished loading, actually." Kess sipped resolutely at her lemonade, but the level in the glass was barely diminishing. "I just need to check the drivers and install a few bits and pieces and we're done."

Finnegan had watched the proceedings of the past hour with interest, from his hiding places under various tables and cabinets. Kess had assembled Mrs Henderson's new computer, and was in the process of installing the operating system. Once she checked all the components and installed a few pieces of software, she could leave. Though, she wondered if Mrs Henderson actually knew how to use a computer.

"What are you planning to do with the computer?" Kess said hesitantly, not wanting to sound rude.

"I thought I might get one of those Instagram thingies. My friend Binty has one, and she gets so many likes. She's always bragging at bridge. I thought, well, if Binty can do it, so can I." She gave Kess a wicked smile.

"Absolutely. Of course you can." Kess set the glass down on the table. She had managed to decrease the volume of lemonade a few centimeters—that would have to do. "I'd better check on it."

Kess walked down the short hallway into the study. The new computer was a fancy piece of kit, with specs that far exceeded anything Mrs Henderson was probably planning to do. Apparently, it had been bought by one of her nephews. "He's very good with all that techno stuff," Mrs Henderson had said. "Has the very latest mobile telephone and all the gizmos." Kess had mentally rolled her eyes. One of the large photos on the mantlepiece had shown a businessman with an obnoxiously know-it-all smirk. "He made a lot on money on these fitness product things. Asked me to invest my savings, but I just don't know." Mrs Henderson had sounded uncertain.

"If you're not sure, get some independent advice. Don't invest just because he says it's a good deal," Kess had said firmly. She hated the thought of this nice woman losing her savings to some skeevy business venture. Kess had scribbled a phone number on a post-it and handed it to Mrs Henderson. "This lady, Holly, helped me set up my business. She can give you some advice. If you mention me, she probably won't even charge just to answer a few questions." Mrs Henderson had nodded thoughtfully and said she'd call. Kess hoped she did. Holly was a no-nonsense financial planner, and her business advice was rock solid.

Kess flicked the mouse and the screen hummed back on. Windows had installed successfully. She scrolled through the list of components and double-checked the drivers and software.

"Do you want me to get rid of any of these?" She indicated the carboard boxes that had housed the various components. Though she built the PCs at her apartment and only did the assembly part in-situ, she liked to give new owners everything that came with the product.

Mrs Henderson nodded. "Whatever I don't need."

Kess checked the internet connection. "What's your Wi-Fi name?"

"Wi-Fi?"

Kess scratched the hair at the base of her neck. "Did your nephew set up the internet for you?"

"I don't know that I have the internet, dear."

"Do you watch Netflix?"

"Oh yes, all the time."

"Where's your landline phone?" Kess had a quick look around the study, but there was no modem or router. She headed back into the corridor.

"In the kitchen." Kess cast about the kitchen until she found the phone. After some further rummaging, she located a small modem-router squished sideways up against the wall behind the toaster. She retrieved it and turned it over.

"Is that what that is?"

"Yep. This is the internet." Kess suppressed a smile. Picking up a biro from a pen-holder on the counter, she wrote the details on the back on her hand. She headed back towards the study. "Mrs Henderson, what were you saying before, about the Family Man?"

"It's been all over the news for weeks, dear. A serial killer. In New England, can you imagine?"

"A serial killer?" Kess sat down and started typing. Was that what the old ladies talked about at bridge? Serial killers? She had thought they would be more interested in crochet and knitting. But then, hadn't she read somewhere that the steady increase in crime fiction sales was driven by elderly women readers? Perhaps there was a book club at bridge. Maybe they had formed one of those old lady detective clubs.

"But he only kills families."

Kess wrinkled her nose as she checked the connection. "I think your internet is good to go. Why only families? That seems weird."

"He's a serial killer," said Mrs Henderson, as though that explained everything. "Would you like another glass of lemonade?"

"No. No. Thank you." Kess checked that the updates were installing correctly. "Do you need me to show you how to use this?" She swept a hand over the computer.

"My nephew said he'd pop around tonight and give me some lessons."

Kess frowned. She wasn't at all sure about this nephew. "I can come back later in the week and show you some stuff if you'd like. No charge."

"Thank you, dear. Maybe that would be best."

"Thursday morning?"

"Yes, lovely."

Kess gathered her things and compiled the unneeded boxes and packets. She made a neat pile of installation disks and manuals, though she doubted Mrs Henderson would use them.

"He's working his way down the coast, you know," nodded Mrs Henderson.

As Kess rose, the old office chair wobbled and creaked, scooting out from beneath her on its rickety wheels. She put a steadying hand on the desk, dislodging the pile of papers she had just made. She sighed, and straightened the papers again. "Who is?"

"The Family Man, dear. The first case was up in Maine. Portland or thereabouts. But the last few nights there have been reports in the Boston area. He's heading south." Mrs Henderson took off her glasses, gave them a rub on the hem of her dress, and placed them back on her nose. If anything, they looked cloudier than before.

Kess frowned. "I'm sure the police will find him soon."

"I hope so. The first few were husbands, wives, and children. But last night they said he killed a gay couple and their two adopted children. Lovely Victorian house in the South End. The theme is definitely families, you see."

It sounded rather ominous, but perhaps the old lady was exaggerating. Too much time on her hands. Kess gave Finnegan another head scratch on the way out. This time he butted against her, rumbling his chest like they were old friends. Mrs Henderson beamed. "See you Thursday, then."

Kess gave the woman a wave as she unlocked her car. Finnegan was winding around Mrs Henderson's legs as she stood on the porch. Kess had a sudden flash, like she was looking at her own life sometime in the future.

She slipped into the driver's seat and started the engine. Her ancient black convertible stuttered and stalled. "Come one." She pumped the pedals and tried again. Finally, the engine roared to life. As she pulled away, she pushed a button on the CD player. Bright pop music spewed from the speakers at full volume. Kess punched another button, and the roof folded away. She pulled the band from her ponytail. The wind fanned her long hair out behind her, blue streaks gleaming electric in the sun. She put on her sunglasses and smiled.

Another beautiful day in New Haven. Blue skies and summer sun and nothing to worry about.

2

Kess saw two more clients and was home by mid-afternoon. Her small business was thriving—there were a lot of elderly residents in the surrounding areas needing computer support. She pushed open the door to her apartment, cardboard component boxes spilling from her arms into the entry. She nudged them aside with one foot and pulled the door closed. Kicking off her shoes, she unloaded the rest of the boxes onto a side table and headed to the bathroom. From there, she made her way into the kitchen where she pulled a box of pizza rolls from the freezer, ripped open the packaging and threw them onto a baking tray. She stuffed the tray into the oven, and set the controls and the timer. Then she pulled open the fridge, grabbed a soda, and looked around. "Grem?" Popping the soda open, she walked around the bench. "Gremlin, where are you?"

The apartment was small and cozy. She had rented the same place for almost ten years. Two bedrooms, with cream walls and hardwood floors. Fireplaces in every room, and a dark Formica kitchen. '80s movie posters were stuck haphazardly on the walls: *Breakfast Club*, *Legend*, *The Last Unicorn*. A few hair metal bands. Dragon figurines, clutching colorful crystals, were lined up along the top of the fireplace. At one end sat a bowl of slightly shriveled fruit and an indoor plant, its leaves drooping sadly towards the floor.

A tiny ball of calico fur flew out of the bedroom and lunged at her ankles. A lively little purr echoed upward. "Hey, there you are." Kess bent down and picked up the small cat with one hand. Gremlin was fully grown, but quite tiny compared to big, fluffy monsters like Finnegan. Kess slung the cat over her shoulder and headed to the lounge, where her impressive custom gaming rig sat against one wall. Gremlin sniffed her shirt, no doubt wondering about the smell of other cat.

Kess set down her beverage and plonked into the plush gaming chair. Gremlin purred from her shoulder. Time to see what the guild was up to. She flicked on the rig. It sprang to life in an array of rainbow colors. Figurines from various cartoons and anime were gathered on the shelves behind the desk. The light reflected eerily off polyvinyl-chloride eyes, as if they were watching. The keyboard oscillated through every color, pulsing as though it was breathing, as did the matching mouse. Kess felt a surge of pride for her computer as it booted up. She pulled on her ironically pink headphones and clicked the mic.

An hour later, the pizza rolls were on a plate, a second soda was half gone, and Kess was deep in a raid. "Jesus, Ben, if you're going to pull half the room at least heal me first!" Kess clicked wildly, and monsters slowly diminished on the screen with pixel-sprays of blood. Discord pinged an alert, and she split-screened the raid to read it. "Guys, I've gotta do a thing, can you pug someone?"

She grinned and clicked the sound off on the headphones, muting the swearing as she teleported out of the raid. Once upon a time, she had gone all out to be accepted and liked by her guild. But she had slowly realized that being herself was better, and ultimately less stressful. Besides, leaving mid-raid was nothing the other members hadn't done to her a million times over at least.

She scrolled through the Discord chat. Kess dabbled in indie software, and her critique partner had sent a detailed bug report for her latest game. Her small pixel games weren't going to make her rich any time soon, but it was a fun pastime. There were surprisingly few errors listed in the notes. Kess launched her software editor and manually debugged the code. Then she tested the game on herself. It was a small text game with pixel graphics; only a half-hour or so to play through. It looked good. Really good. Kess felt a wash of satisfaction.

As she finished the last pizza roll, Kess uploaded her game. Then she started a new thread. Kesswing78 New Game—*Save the Fawn*. It was a sweet little game about rescuing a baby deer from an evil witch's enchanted forest. It had several options to win, like tying balloons to the deer and floating it out, or building a raft and sending it down a river. There was even a magic portal, if you reached the edge of the forest. But if the witch caught the player character or the deer, it was game over.

Kess was part of a community that would play through the game and give feedback before she launched the game on her main site. She always got the jitters when she uploaded a new game. Waiting for people to finish their first playthrough and leave comments. It was nerve-wracking. Best to keep busy. Kess fed Gremlin. Then she grabbed her laptop and headed out.

Her condo was down near the harbor, in a nice neighborhood. She could walk along the quiet, tree-lined residential streets near the water, or head into downtown New Haven, a bustling area full of students and shops. The harbor was quieter than downtown, and though her living room window looked out onto the other condos, from her kitchen she had glimpses of the water all the way to Long Island Sound. All in all, it was an easy place to live.

There was a diner nearby and an oyster bar down the street, but the trendy coffee shops were mostly downtown which was about a thirty-minute walk. Kess wanted to clear her head, so that's where she was going.

As she walked the pavement past pretty houses, hands buried deep in the pockets of her light-grey hoodie, she couldn't help the feeling she was being watched. The hairs on the back of her neck prickled. But there was no one around. It was late afternoon. A few mothers with prams, heading home from the local park. A couple of teenagers sitting along the brick wall in front of an apartment block, sharing a cigarette back and forth. Nothing unusual.

As she crossed into the downtown district, there was more life. A comforting hustle of shoppers, students, and various business people. Kess reached her favorite coffee shop, *Cinnamon & Salt*, without incident. After she ordered, she found a booth right in the back. In the semi-dark, she cracked open her laptop and started typing.

When her coffee arrived, she almost jumped out of her seat.

"Sorry," said the waitress nervously, placing a large, brown mug beside her. The coffee was sprinkled with cinnamon sugar across a heart shaped into the foam. "I like your hair."

Kess fingered the long, blue strands escaping from under her hood. "Thanks."

"What are you working on?"

The waitress was a teenager—short, blonde-dyed hair, dark skin, and a metal nose ring. She was chewing gum and looked friendly enough. Kess fiddled with her hair. "I write fan fiction."

"No way. What kind?" The waitress hovered like she wanted to sit down and chat. Her name tag said her name was Kelly.

"It's...slash fiction. You know... Same sex, romance-type stuff."

"Yeah. I freaking love AO3, hey." Kelly grinned and blew a pink bubble.

"I write there a bit, under *Kesswing*. Check me out sometime."

"Yeah man, I totally will." Kelly looked over towards the counter.

"Oh geez, boss is watching. Good luck with it." She gave Kess a wink and sauntered away.

Kess returned to the page of fiction scrolling across her screen. A minute later, someone slid into the seat opposite. She looked up, fully expecting it to be Kelly back for more gossip. But it was a stranger, a woman. There were plenty of free seats in the coffee shop, the woman must have sat next to her on purpose. Kess's heart thumped in surprise. "Can I help you?"

The woman was dressed in linen pants and a trim jacket, smart but casual. She had chin-length, flaming red hair, brown eyes, and elegant make-up that accentuated high cheek bones and full lips. Her expensive-looking jewelry clunked against the table as she tapped her fingers. "You don't know me, but I know you. Ms Hawkins."

Kess narrowed her eyes. "I'm sorry, what?"

The woman looked flustered. Her glitter-edged fingernails tapped wildly on the tabletop. "That was supposed to come off as deeply mysterious, but it was just downright creepy, right."

"Yep."

"Sorry, I'm new at this."

"At what?"

"Investigative journalism." The woman rummaged in her candy-pink purse and produced a business card, which she swept across the table. Her name was Michelle and she apparently worked for the West Haven Chronicle. "It's Mish, for short. And your name is Kess? Short for…?"

"It's just Kess."

"Just Kess? Oh, I like that, simple but powerful. Well, I'm pleased to meet you, Kess." Mish waved her hand in the air, bracelets jangling, to summon Kelly. When she caught the girl's attention, she ordered a small cappuccino: low fat, lots of foam.

Kess screwed up her face. "Why would the West Haven Chronicle want to talk to me?"

"We don't. Not officially. This is off the books." Mish lowered her voice to a whisper. "I'm researching a super important story and I think I might need your help."

"I think you have the wrong person. But anyway, what are you researching?"

Mish settled herself in the chair. "Have you heard of the Family Man?"

"The serial killer?" Her voice came out louder than she meant, and Mish waved wildly at her to be quiet.

"Sorry."

They sat silently for a moment. Kess had initially taken Mish to be about the same age as her. But under closer examination, the make-up made her look older than she was. She was probably still in her twenties. Why on earth did she want to talk to Kess? She didn't know anything about the Family Man, she'd only just heard of him this morning.

The cappuccino arrived and Mish took a hasty sip, spilling foamy coffee over the sides of the mug. Kess wondered if this bundle of nervous energy really needed more caffeine. But her curiosity was piqued despite herself. She couldn't resist a good mystery. If Kess was better with people, she probably would have considered studying journalism herself.

"You call this lots of foam?" Mish waved Kelly away with a sigh and took another sip. "It's good, though."

"The coffee is great. That's why I write here. So…the Family Man?"

"I'm trying to find out who he is," said Mish, with a melodramatic pause.

"Aren't the police already working on that?"

"Indubitably. But I found a clue to a place that doesn't really exist anymore. Or at least, it's been closed down. An orphanage. I'm trying to trace its previous denizens. You were adopted, right?"

Kess blinked in surprise, then annoyance. "I was in foster care, but never an orphanage."

"Are you sure?"

Kess closed her laptop with a clack. "Who are you? Really? What is this all about?"

Mish fished in her purse, then slid a torn photograph across the table. "I had a friend in the force run this through facial recognition. It's you. When you were like, ten."

"Facial recognition?" This day was getting weird. Really, really weird. Kess wound strands of blue hair tight around her fingers. When she pulled on her hair, the tingling pain in her scalp helped her focus. It was an old habit.

"Red light camera." Mish grinned. That seemed plausible. Kess and her convertible got plenty of tickets.

Kess plucked up the photo and held it in the light. The photo showed a small boy and girl, and half of another child. It was torn roughly down the edges. The girl had long dark hair and a stony expression. The boy was softer, rounder. Younger perhaps. The eyes staring out of the photo, from the face of the girl, were Kess's eyes. She had no photos of herself at this age, no way to be sure. But looking at the girl, she was inclined to believe that Mish was right. The picture was of her. "Where did you get this?"

"From the orphanage. It's been closed down, but the door wasn't locked. I found this. That's you, right?"

"Maybe."

"And the boy?"

Kess shook her head. "I don't know him." Something plucked at her memory. Three children. A building. A dark place. But she had never been in an orphanage, as far as she knew. "Where did you say this orphanage was?"

"It's a bit of a drive out of town. Up in Aylesbury. Past the old chemical plant, there's a housing estate. Built back in the 70's, I think. The orphanage must have been one of those old Victorian mansions—I mean, there are historic buildings dotted all over New Haven, right? Anyway, this one is within the estate, but it's alone up on a hill. Willow Hill. They call it Willow Close."

"Willow Close?" A shudder worked its way down Kess's spine.

"It's the name of the main street in the housing estate, so not exactly an original name, but a lot of those old buildings are named for the streets they…"

Kess had stopped listening. She was lost in a howling, writhing surge of memories. Blood and knives. The incessant whine of a drill. Death. So much death. A crack in the wall with shadows and light. And a dark place. A very dark place.

3

She couldn't breathe. Her lungs were burning and she couldn't see. Everything was cold and murky. Freezing. She was in the water. It pressed in around her. Dark and cold. Stifling, smothering. What had happened? She thought, perhaps, she had been in a car. Was she still in the car? Her head hurt, a dull throb beneath the cold. Her thoughts were cascading, confused. Blackness, at the edges of her mind, pushed to consume her. She flung her arms out, feeling around her. She hit something solid. A window? Beyond the window, water swirled and bubbled. Wherever she was, it was sinking, and fast. She tried to take a breath. Water surged into her lungs. She couldn't cough it out, the water was all around her. Choking. Suffocating. Her eyes peered and strained, trying to acclimatize to the murk. Trying to see, anything. There was a body beside her. She pushed her hands towards it. A boy. He was moving, flailing. She grabbed his arm. He turned his face to hers, eyes white and rolling in his head. She had to…they had to…get out. Had to get out…out of here…out of the water. She took another breath. Water burned and flowed. Consciousness ebbed. She was drowning. Drowning. Dying.

Kess woke, gasping for air. Clawing at her throat in the dark of her room. Her heart pounded. From somewhere beyond the room came a small miaow. Gremlin. Kess fought her eyes open. Everything was silent. There was no water flooding her room. It was calm, normal. She pushed upright in bed. The sheets felt too close, stifling. She rearranged them, over and over, trying to calm down.

The door shuddered slightly, and a few seconds later a bundle of calico launched onto the blankets. Gremlin stalked up the bed and butted against her face. She grabbed the cat and held her. "I was drowning." Gremlin purred, the soft rumble familiar and reassuring in the dark. Kess lay down again, heart thumping. Gremlin curled up on her chest, and she fell back into a restless sleep. When she woke again, Gremlin was gone. The sun was shining through the windows, and the phone was ringing.

Kess felt groggy, still discombobulated from the dream. She swung her legs over the bed into purple unicorn slippers, and wandered into the living room. Rubbing her eyes, she unplugged her phone from the charger and swiped a finger across the screen to answer. "Hello?"

"We found him."

"What? Who is this?"

"Oh, sorry, this is Mish. We found him, the boy in the photograph."

Kess frowned. Her brain was still swimming in the dream and she was getting a headache. She tried to focus. The photograph in the coffee shop. Her and a boy. Familiar somehow. The orphanage at Willow Close. "Who is he?"

"His name is David Collier. He's an elementary school teacher. I'm going to meet with him this afternoon. You should come."

"I don't know." Kess rubbed her eyes ferociously as she opened the fridge. She rummaged for a soda, popped it open, and downed half of it. The icy liquid fizzed down her throat and fought the headache away.

Her mind flashed to the sensation of liquid being sucked into her lungs, of drowning. The soda caught in her throat. A mouthful fizzed back up and out, onto the floor. "Damnit." She put down the soda and grabbed a dish towel, gripping the phone between her shoulder and ear. Mish was extolling the importance of the meeting, but she had stopped listening. As she bent over, the headache returned, thumping soundly against her left eyeball. She mopped up the soda, listening to Mish's instructions, and rang off as soon as possible.

Taking a deep breath, Kess crossed the floor and sank onto the sofa. Mish wanted to go this afternoon, at half past three. Just after school finished. She said they should corner him in his classroom and ask some questions. It seemed like a badly thought-out plan, but Kess was too tired to argue. Her eyes closed for a moment, red light flickering behind her eyelids. She fought her eyes open. What even was the time? She checked her phone. The clock said it was already close to midday. The dream had really messed with her. And now she had to go meet some school teacher? She had no client bookings. It was her day off. What did she have to lose? Kess sank back into the sofa and flicked on the TV. A reality program. The drone of sounds and voices calmed her thoughts. In the background of her mind, water swirled and bubbled.

The school corridor was bustling with students. Children with color-ful backpacks rushed through the halls to meet parents. Others stood talking loudly with friends. The bell had rung maybe fifteen minutes ago. Kess and Mish had stopped at the principal's office, where a stern, middle-aged woman called Ms Robinson lurked behind a steel desk, leafing through a large binder. They had been pointed, in due course and with a measure of skepticism, to the relevant classroom. Now they waited outside. There were still a few students lingering in the room, and they wanted to catch Mr Collier alone.

The school smelled, as schools often do, of a strange mixture of dried paint, canteen food, and imprisonment. On the far wall a row of closed, beige lockers stood stoically. Kess had been trying to remember her own school days, but it was a blur. She barely remembered anything before the middle of high school. Just flashes of memory. Inconsistent pieces.

Mish fidgeted next to her. The ends of her bright red hair curled elegantly out from below her chin. Her make-up was flawless. Kess admired the attention to detail; she felt ragged by comparison. She had a brief flash of envy: Mish probably had an easy time at school, being so outgoing and fashionable. Kess had secretly both admired and hated those kids, the ones who seemed effortlessly put together. Imagine knowing exactly what you wanted from life so early on, and here Kess was still trying to figure it out.

"Were you popular?" The thought spilled out of her mouth before Kess could stop it. With her seemingly innate sense of style, Mish had to have been one of those popular kids. Hell, she had probably been Homecoming Queen. From what Kess could remember of her own school days, she had been practically invisible. Yet the child in the photo looked strong, confident. It pulled at her, this life she could not remember. What if she was different back then?

"I'm sorry?" Mish was looking at her with raised eyebrows.

"Back in school, I mean. You seem so…stylish. I was just thinking about my own school days. I don't think anyone even knew I existed. I would never have admitted it but, to be honest, sometimes I wished I had more style."

A wistful expression crossed Mish's face. "That's funny in a way. Back then, I wished no one noticed me."

It was Kess' turn to frown. Why would Mish want that? Had her school days been difficult, after all? "I just assumed you would have been really popular… I'm sorry if that was wrong, I…it's that darn photo, I keep trying to remember my old life and I just can't."

Mish smoothed her perfect hair and shifted uncomfortably. "I don't have any childhood photos either. Nothing before my eighteenth birthday, actually." She cleared her throat. "You can't remember your old life and I don't want to remember mine. It...doesn't feel like me at all." She chewed her lip, obviously aware Kess wasn't following. "I wanted to tell you, but you never know how people are going to react, you know?" She cleared her throat again, nervously. "I'm trans, actually."

"Oh, really?" Kess flicked her eyes back to the beige lockers, wondering what she should say. It didn't matter to her how someone identified, what gender they wanted to be. People could live their lives however they wanted, as far as she was concerned.

"It was difficult," said Mish slowly, "trying to work out why I felt the way I did. Not fitting in and not knowing why. You think I'm stylish, but back then I was just awkward...and bullied."

"I'm really sorry," said Kess quickly, acutely embarrassed by the assumptions she had made. She could feel her face reddening. "That's... that must have been a lot to process." Mish had obviously had a pretty hard time in school, trying to figure things out. "And here I was thinking you would have been Homecoming Queen, for sure."

"Girl, I wish."

There was an awkward silence. Kess wrapped a strand of blue hair around her finger. "So, you transitioned after high school?"

"Mmhm. It doesn't bother you?" Mish pressed, obviously worried.

"No, of course not." Kess said quickly, trying to think of the words to express her certainty that people could be whoever they wanted. If anything, this explained the flawless hair and make-up, the glitzy fashion. Mish was probably overcompensating. Then again, it suited her over-the-top personality. She was still staring at Kess, probably waiting for a better response. Kess met Mish's eyes with what she hoped was a reassuring smile. "I believe that people should be whoever they want. Everyone deserves the chance to live in a way that is authentic and meaningful, to be true to themselves..." She rubbed the base of her neck. "Uh...has it been very difficult, since then?"

"Yes," said Mish like it was a big understatement. "But it's worth all the trouble to finally be myself."

Kess felt a twinge deep inside. Maybe everyone was just trying to figure things out, all the time. Maybe even those really put-together kids had their own stuff to worry about, the same as everyone else. It was a bad idea to judge people before you knew them, but it was hard to avoid sometimes. Kess shook her head. "It's not easy being a woman," she said wryly. "But...welcome to the club, I guess?"

Mish visibly relaxed. "Thank you."

That conversation was probably never easy. It must be hard not knowing how people might react. Feeling like you had something to explain, all the time, like a heavy weight. She felt bad that Mish might think she was under pressure to have that conversation. At the same time, she was curious about the logistics. Not curious enough to ask, though. Mish might hate personal questions as much as she did.

"That's the last of them, let's go." Mish grabbed her arm and tugged her into the classroom. Kess's heart thumped at the sudden change of pace. She tried to refocus her brain on the situation at hand. Why was she going along with this strange trip? What were they even going to say to this guy?

David Collier was a round man with sandy hair that fell over hazel, button eyes. He was peering through wire spectacles at a stack of papers on his desk. He looked roughly the same age as Kess. The room was draped with colorful children's art: handprints and animals and flowers. Guinea pigs were lazily turning on a wheel in a white cage at the back of the room. Plants grew from pots along the windowsills.

When he noticed he was being observed, the teacher straightened in his chair and peered at them, curious. "Can I help you?"

"Mr Collier?"

"Yes. David."

"I'm Mish and this is Kess. We're thinking about placing our boy, our precious angel, Timothy, at this school, and Ms Robinson suggested we speak with you."

Kess's heart sped into a straight canter at the audacity of the lie. A little warning would have been nice. Mish linked arms with her and leaned in, giving her a loving glance and a nudge.

"Yep. That is correct," said Kess awkwardly. She could feel Mish inwardly roll her eyes.

"And how old is Timothy?"

"Eight," said Mish firmly after a slight pause and, presumably, some mental arithmetic.

"A bit old for second grade. Is there any reason you wouldn't rather place him with Mrs Lovecraft, in third?" A polite way of asking whether *our precious, fictitious angel, Timothy*, was a delayed learner.

"He's only seven," Kess nudged Mish back with what she hoped was a sufficiently loving look. "Honestly, this one would lose her head if it wasn't screwed on."

Mish gave an over-the-top giggle. "Sorry, I was thinking of his sister, Amelie."

"You have two children?"

"Absolutely."

"Seven and eight?"

"Yes?" Mish's forced laughter faltered. Kess mentally rolled her eyes. This was going every bit as terribly as she would have predicted. She still had a headache thrumming behind her eyes. She wanted to be at home, asleep on the sofa in front of the TV, not dragged into all this weirdness. Yet, here they were.

David Collier took off his glasses, placed them carefully on top of his students' papers, and pinched the bridge of his nose. "What is this really about?"

"We're sorry to have wasted your time," said Kess firmly, trying to drag Mish out of the room. But she was stood fast, not to be moved. "Let's go," Kess implored, an edge creeping into her voice. Could you get arrested for impersonating a couple? For inventing two school aged children? She didn't want to find out.

Mish shook her off and approached the desk. "I'm sorry. It was stupid to lie. It's just, the truth is a bit strange."

"Well," David folded his arms. "You certainly have my attention. What is it that you want?"

Kess dithered where she stood. The more David Collier spoke, the more she felt she knew him from somewhere. She wanted to leave, but curiosity was fast overtaking her better judgement. Besides, he didn't seem angry with them, more bemused. She hesitantly stepped forward, to stand next to Mish.

"Do I know you?" Collier peered up at her as she approached. "You look familiar."

Kess wound a strand of blue hair around her finger. "I'm not sure."

Mish pulled the photograph out of her purse, and placed it on top of the pile of student work, right in front of David Collier. He picked it up carefully, by the edges, and stared. "What is this?"

"Do you recognize it?"

David shook his head. "Where was this taken? Who are these children?"

"It's a photo I found in an old, abandoned orphanage. The girl is Kess. The boy…well, to be honest, my information says that it's you."

He scratched at his nose. "Well now. I don't think it can be me. Though, the eyes do look like mine." It was true: the hazel eyes staring out from under the sandy, blond hair in the photo looked a lot like his. He held the photo up, to compare the girl with Kess. "Yes, I can see your likeness here. But I feel as though I would remember, if we had met. Besides, I've never even been in an orphanage, let alone grown up in one. Where did you say the place was?"

"It's called Willow Close."

A shadow passed across David Collier's face, like he was remembering something deep and dark and forgotten. "He always killed the deer," he whispered, in a trance-like voice.

"What?" Mish's eyes went wide. Kess's heart stopped in her throat.

David's eyes refocused and he blinked a few times. "I'm sorry, what were you saying?"

"You said something, just now."

"Did I?" His eyes went blank again, just for a second. Then the moment passed and he handed back the photograph. Mish put it away in her purse, closing the clasp with a snap. "Are you sure you don't remember anything? About the orphanage?"

He shook his head. "What is this all about, anyway?"

"Part of an investigation, for the *West Haven Chronicle*."

"You're a journalist?"

Mish inclined her head. Her eyes gleamed. "I'm working on a really exciting story…"

"We should get going. We've taken up enough of your time," said Kess hastily. She suddenly felt like it was a bad idea to tell anyone what they were working on. Or to mention the Family Man.

"If you remember anything, or want to talk…" Mish handed David a business card. "Thank you for your time," she said over her shoulder as Kess hustled her out of the room.

When they were back in the corridor, Mish glared at her. "That was rude. Didn't you want to wait and see if he remembered? I mean, the way he looked at that photo. It meant something to him."

"Maybe." Kess headed away down the corridor, towards the exit. Mish trotted to catch up.

"We shouldn't have rushed out like that. He probably won't want to talk to us again now."

"I don't think you should tell him that you're researching the Family Man," Kess blurted as they walked. "It could be dangerous. I don't think you should tell anyone."

"David Collier is not exactly a threat. You saw him. He teaches kids. They still do hand painting for goodness sake!"

"Even so. We don't know anything about him."

Kess couldn't shake the feeling she knew him. But from where? The photograph still felt as unfamiliar as the boy in it. But when she'd looked at David Collier, her throat had closed up and she felt like she was drowning. That seemed like a bad sign. *He always killed the deer.* That was what he had murmured when he looked at the photograph. It may not have meant anything to Mish, but it meant something to her. She just wished she knew what. She had fragments of a memory. Flickers of a deer in a forest. A hunter. However hard she chased the thought in her mind, she could not remember the details. But it felt dark and desperate, and dangerous.

Mish grabbed her arm and pulled her to a stop. "You know something. You remember him, don't you?" Her eyes were on fire.

"No. not exactly," Kess sighed with frustration. "I don't know what I remember."

"But there's something there."

"Maybe. Look, don't tell anyone anything, until we know more. That's all I'm saying."

Kess took off along the corridor again, pushing through the heavy exit doors with Mish hard on her heels. They burst through into the cool of the air outside and paused. Birds twittered overhead, and kids yelled obscenities in the playground. The sun's rays were a warm relief to the cool breeze.

"Alright. So, what do we do now?" Mish sounded equal parts exasperated and intrigued.

Kess swallowed. "I can't believe I'm about to say this… I think you need to take me to see this orphanage."

4

They took Mish's car, leaving Kess's parked up the street from her condo. "I'm not sure yours would make it," Mish had said, not unkindly, while staring at Kess's battered convertible. Mish drove a flashy, deep blue SUV. A rather expensive car for a journalist, Kess thought. The car hummed along the road with an eerie precision. The absence of engine noise would have been disconcerting, but Mish had docked her iPhone and the Bluetooth was blasting out *Uprising* by Muse.

"I love this intro! Kinda sounds like Dr Who, don't you think?"

"Sure." Kess watched the scenery flashing by outside the window. Mish drove fast. Really fast. At least the thrill of the speed took her mind off the decision to go to an abandoned orphanage, out of town, with a woman she barely knew. Willow Close. Why did the very name send shivers down her spine? In her mind's eye, she pictured a house, tattered and whitewashed. A creaking gate. A hand with bleeding knuckles, stretching out…

"How much do you know about Malvan? The incident back in the '80s?" Mish's question broke into her daydream.

"What?" Kess turned back from the window. Even late in the day, Mish was as perfectly groomed as ever. Her hair curled neatly against the collar of her smart, blue-dotted dress, and she was wearing dark eyelashes that set off her warm brown eyes.

Mish flicked her eyes sideways, registered Kess's lack of comprehension, and pointed a polished nail toward a wide, empty tract of land, and an unfamiliar building that looked like an abandoned powerplant. It crouched, twisted metal and low buildings, ominous against the darkening sky.

"I've never been up here before."

"It's an old chemical plant. Malvan Chemicals. Closed a long time ago."

"After the incident in the '80s?" Kess repeated Mish's words.

"Right. There was a spill. The chemicals got into the air and spread over the town in a big toxic cloud, settling on people's houses, in their yards. It was a huge mess. The plant was shut down soon after. The owners did a flit, I think, to avoid prosecution. It wasn't just the contamination. There were deaths."

"Deaths?" Kess stared in the rear-view mirror. The chemical plant hulked like a metal beast. In front of the buildings, at the side of the road, she could make out something standing. It looked like a person. A figure in a hood.

"Who is that?"

Mish followed Kess's gaze and looked in the rear-view. "I don't see anyone."

When Kess looked again, the figure was gone. The image burned on the backs of her eyelids, a man in a hood, watching. The back of her neck prickled. Who was he? Had she imagined him?

Mish cleared her throat. "There were several deaths in the town, around the same time as the chemical leak. But since the place was closed down, they weren't pursued. Not in depth."

"So, people were poisoned? By the chemicals?"

"People got sick after—and those cases were litigated, as far as I know. But at the actual time, the same week as the spill, there was a string of unexplained deaths."

Kess turned in her seat to look at Mish. "You mean murders?" Was this all somehow connected to the Family Man?

"Not exactly." Mish kept her eyes on the road, and her neck bobbed as she swallowed. "The deaths were violent, but as far as anyone could tell, the injuries were self-inflicted."

"Self-inflicted. What, like...suicides?"

"I don't think anyone ever really made the connection that the chemicals might have made people harm themselves. The fallout from the spill caused too much chaos. Then there were the subsequent cases of sickness. But I think Malvan was to blame for those other deaths, too."

"Let me get this straight: you're investigating a series of strange deaths that happened around the same time as a chemical spill, back in the '80s? What does any of that have to do with..."

"While I was chasing down the old files from the chemical plant, investigating the incident, I found a link with the Family Man."

"But you just said the deaths were self-inflicted."

"It's complicated. The spill also led me to Willow Close."

"What does a chemical spill have to do with an orphanage?"

"Like I said, it's complicated."

Kess leaned her head against the cool of the passenger side window. The headache thrummed behind her eyeballs. "What does any of this have to do with me?"

"I'm not sure. Have you always lived in New Haven?"

"I was raised in Boston. I came down here for school."

"College?"

"Yeah. Studying IT."

"Couldn't you have stayed—in Boston, I mean?"

"Sure. But to be honest, I wanted to get away."

"From your family?"

"Foster family. There's nothing wrong with them. I just wanted… something of my own, I guess."

Kess frowned against the window. She had never been mistreated in care, nothing untoward. But she had bounced from family to family before settling with the one in Boston. That had been as part of a large foster family, with people coming and going all the time. New Haven, her little condo at the harbor, Gremlin—it was stability. It was one thing that was all hers.

"How about you?" Kess swiveled her eyes back to Mish.

"My family?"

Kess nodded. Mish checked the mirrors, and adjusted their speed as she answered. "I was adopted as a baby. They were always up front about that. But they love me like their own, and to me they've always been my real Mom and Dad, you know. I have my own place in town, and they still live in the family house over in East Rock. I see them all the time. And Sunday dinner, every week. Maybe you should come with me sometime."

"Nice neighborhood." East Rock. The car, the clothes, the place downtown. It was starting to make sense. Mish's parents obviously had money. A lot of money. She didn't seem stuck-up about it, not like other country club patrons Kess had met. In Kess's experience, her blue hair, gender neutral clothes, and IT skills meant the rich, fashionable set never really gave her the time of day. Not that she cared. She wondered what Mish's rich parents had thought about her transitioning.

Mish seemingly read her mind. Perhaps she was used to people wondering. "They were very supportive of the change," she said quickly, running a hand self-consciously through her hair, re-curling the ends.

"Cool." Kess turned back to the window and closed her eyes against the glass. She didn't want to make Mish uncomfortable, or to feel like she had to answer awkward questions. The details were none of her business. Besides, the headache was intensifying. She should have gone home, to sleep. But she was too curious now, about the orphanage, the chemical plant. The incident. The unexplained deaths. Why did it all have such a familiar ring to it? She saw again in her mind the hand with bloody knuckles reaching out towards a rusty gate.

"If you want to ask questions about me, that's fine."

"Thanks. Maybe I will, but not today."

"We have enough to worry about, right?" The car slowed to a stop. "We're here."

Kess opened her eyes, butterflies fluttering in her stomach. From the car window, she took her first look at Willow Close. It was imposing: a huge, Victorian mansion crouched on a hill.

Kess got out of the car slowly, a ball of apprehension kneading her stomach. She stared up at the building. It was large and gothic looking, made of thick walls and arched windows. Three stories high, by the look of it, with a single tower rising a floor higher—an attic, perhaps. There were gables and top floor windows with pointed arches. Balconies stretched from several portions of the upper building. The whole monstrosity had a pale-rose hue to the brickwork. Lawns, which had presumably once been deliberately manicured, were now patchy and unkempt. Dust and dead grass sat either side of a weed-studded path. A set of wide steps, flanked by intricate columns, led to the main door.

A dusty sign hanging from brickwork announced the name of the place as Willow Close Care Home. 1 Willow Close, Aylesbury.

"Willow Close." A shiver ran the length of Kess's spine as she said the name. But she felt no closer to remembering this strange place.

"Does it look familiar?"

She shook her head. "Not really."

"Perhaps if we try inside?"

"You want to go in there?" Kess frowned. The sky was fast turning to night. She hadn't given much thought to the time when suggesting they come. They had left the school, stopped for coffee, and then stopped again to sort out their cars. It had taken the best part of an hour to drive up here. The sun had set on the way. It was basically nighttime, and they were alone in the dark outside an abandoned building. A huge, gothic building, linked to a deranged serial killer, which exuded a definite, haunted house vibe. It suddenly all seemed like a bad idea.

Mish was rummaging in the boot of the car. She emerged with a huge, yellow flashlight. "I'm a journalist. Always prepared. And yeah, I want to go in there."

She grabbed Kess's arm before she could protest further, and together they walked towards Willow Close.

The imposing walnut door creaked ominously as they pushed it open. Kess had half-hoped it would be locked, but there was no sign of any security. The building was simply empty. The entrance hall must once have been very grand; black and white tiles lined the floor, and a sweeping, black walnut staircase ascended to the upper levels. Chandeliers hung from the ceiling, unlit and dusty. Cobwebs dangled from corners and doorways.

As the door thumped against the brickwork, making them flinch, there was a screech. Something took off from the chandelier and flew straight at them. Mish waved the flashlight and the thing veered, wings beating furiously. Kess felt wingtips trail the top of her head as it skimmed over her and vanished into the night.

"What was that?" she asked, trying to maintain an outward appearance of calm while her heart thundered.

"A bat, maybe?" Mish straightened the collar of her dress. Kess ran a hand over the top of her own head, where the thing's silken wings had brushed against her. They walked cautiously forward, peering around in case of any other creatures. Each step left a print in the dust on the floor. Doorways opened to the left and right of the main hall. Rooms that might once have been grand were now left to decay.

Mish shone her flashlight into the first room on the left. "Some sort of school room," she concluded.

"Same with this one." Kess noted, using the light from her phone to assess the room to the right. A row of pews faced a lectern at the front. "Bedrooms are probably upstairs," she said. Mish gave her a sharp look, and she added quickly, "Just a guess."

"You're right. Bedrooms upstairs, kitchen and admin offices to the back," said Mish. At Kess's look, she said "I've been here before, remember? But I never looked twice in these front rooms."

"Where did you find the photo?"

"Over here."

Kess followed Mish down the hall to stand in front of a noticeboard. Fading newspaper clippings and class photos were pinned to the board. Students and teachers. Memos of various accomplishments and old announcements.

"It was pinned just here." Mish pointed to a small space, below a faded clipping from the West Haven Chronicle. The article announced a mathematics prize that had been awarded to several of the students. Kess felt as though she had heard their names before somewhere. "Does anything look familiar? Anyone?" A trophy case stood next to the noticeboard. Willow Close had produced some exceptional students in its time. Was she one of them?

"Looks like a lot of them were pretty successful." Kess said with a snort as she perused the clippings and trophies.

"There were persistent rumors about why this place was closed down."

"Rumors?"

"They aren't pleasant. It was said that teachers abused the kids here. Nothing sexual. But severe punishments for poor achievement or misbehavior. Beatings, and psychological stuff like locking them in the dark. It's how they forced them to excel."

Kess remembered the photo Mish had shown her. The blank eyes staring out. If she had been here at Willow Close, had she been abused, severely punished? Is that why she didn't remember? Kess looked again at the faces on the board. Pale, solemn eyes stared back.

"And then there were the deaths." Mish's tone was somber.

"From the chemical spill?"

Mish shook her head. "These were later, a few years after. Several of the students died here. I found out during my research. Perhaps it was covered up at the time. Though, this place was closed not long after."

"It's been vacant all these years?"

"It's a historic building, but I don't think anyone wanted to take on the history, or the renovation bill."

Kess stared at the children on the noticeboard. "Why did you take that photo in particular? When there are all these others."

"In the photo, there's another boy whose face you can only half see. I hoped you two might know him."

"How does this all connect with Malvan Chemicals, and with the Family Man?" Kess said the name with a whisper. In the dark of the building, it seemed unlucky to give voice to a name like that. The darkness pressed in, cold and tight around them.

"I was tracing the families who were killed. There was one case in particular where a child survived, a boy. He was sent here, after his parents died. My original story was about the spill and its effects. I thought maybe I could find the boy and get a first-hand account. He'd be grown up now, but he must still remember. No one would forget a thing like that, right? That was my thinking."

"You think he's the other boy in the photo?"

"Yes."

Kess studied the noticeboard. She did not recognize any of the faces that stared back from clippings or photos. Had she really been here? The place felt creepy, but it was an abandoned orphanage at night. Possibly full of roosting bats. The creepy vibe was to be expected. It felt like the setting from every horror movie ever. She couldn't say whether she had been here before. The creepiness outweighed any instincts she might have had about the place. But why was Mish talking in past tense about her search for the survivor of the spill? As though she'd stopped looking for him.

"What changed?"

"I found out how they were killed."

"The boy's parents?"

Mish didn't answer. She had been roaming around the hall as she talked. Now she was stopped somewhere behind the staircase. "Take a look at this." Kess crossed to where her voice was coming from. Mish had edged around behind the stairs. In the corner was a small metal door. "What do you think is down there?"

"You know in horror movies, where you end up shouting at the screen: 'don't go down there'?"

"Yeah."

"I think that's what's down there."

Mish shone the flashlight under her chin, so her face glowed with pale light. "Are you scared?"

"Aren't you?"

Mish flicked her hair. "I mean, not really. We're the only ones here." As she said it, the entrance door gave a resounding creak, and a light shone into the foyer. Mish turned off her flashlight and grabbed Kess's hand, pulling her under the stairs. They crouched and squeezed themselves into the space. Dust swirled around them. Kess put a hand across her mouth, trying not to sneeze. Footsteps thudded across the floor. The light swung back and forth.

"Who is it?" Kess whispered, voice muffled by her hand. "Security?"

"I hope so." Mish whispered into her ear. "Better in trouble than murdered."

"Murdered? Why would…" Kess stopped talking. Her heart thumped in her chest. Pain shot down her side and her stomach clenched in knots.

She knew exactly who Mish was afraid of. The Family Man.

The footsteps went down the corridor towards the noticeboard.

"Should we run for the car?" Mish's whisper was urgent. Kess couldn't decide. It depended on the speed of the person with the light. There was no way to judge whether it was safer to stay or run. The footsteps echoed towards the kitchen.

"Come on." Mish grabbed Kess and hauled her out from under the stairs. They were pushing to their feet when the light swung sharply towards them. "Back! Get back!" Mish whispered, shoving Kess back under the stairs and scrambling after her. They huddled together, with arms linked and heads pressed together. Their hot breaths mingled in the cold.

"Give me the flashlight," whispered Kess, grabbing for it. Mish relinquished the heavy flashlight as the footsteps came back towards them. Kess readied it as a weapon. She wasn't about to get murdered without a fight.

The light swung down and ran along the wall to the tiny metal door, then it crept, inch by inch, under the stairs, a glowing puddle spreading across the floor, until it found their shoes. Slowly, painfully, the light swung upwards to reveal their faces.

"Come out," said a male voice.

Grabbing each other, Mish and Kess clambered out from under the stairs, in a whirl of dust, to stand in the hallway. Mish sneezed and blocked her eyes from the light. Kess gripped the flashlight hard.

"You two?" The light swung away from them, to highlight its owner. In the glare, they could see the light came from a mobile phone. The hand holding the phone was attached to David Collier. He was frowning at them, obviously confused. "What are you doing here?"

Kess glared at him, still brandishing the flashlight. "What are *you* doing here?"

David held up his hands. He popped the phone into his shirt pocket, where its glow was muted but enough to light the immediate surrounds. "After your visit, I couldn't get this address out of my head. I was compelled to see it for myself."

"You scared us half to death. We thought you were the…" Kess nudged Mish hard, before she could say the name. "We thought you were going to murder us," she covered, lamely.

"I can see why. This place is quite the stuff of horror movies." David looked around appraisingly. He pointed over to the wall. "What do you think is down there?" Kess knew without looking, that he was pointing at the metal door behind the stairs. She felt drawn to it too.

But she didn't particularly want to venture into the basement of the place, in the middle of the night, with two people she didn't know. That seemed wildly unsafe.

Mish nudged her arm. "We should go look."

David had already gone over to the door. He pulled on it. The door creaked open. He took his phone out of his pocket and shone its light. "Stairs." He looked back to them, questioning.

Kess grabbed Mish and pulled her out of earshot. "Do you really want to go down a creepy staircase, into the basement, with some guy we've only just met?"

Mish raised her eyebrows. "He's harmless."

Kess tightened her grip and leaned in close. "For all you know, *he* could be the Family Man." She felt Mish shiver.

"I'm going to have a look." David Collier called amiably. He gave them a little wave, and then disappeared down the stairs behind the metal door.

Mish and Kess stood on the black and white tiles, unsure what to do. "Do you have any weapons?" asked Kess. She flicked on the flashlight and held it pointed at the ground, where it made a bright circle on the tiles.

Mish gave her a look. "No. Do you?"

"No."

"Come check this out!" David's voice echoed up to where they were standing. He sounded excited, rather than potentially murderous. But there was no way to be sure. They looked at each other.

"I mean…we came all the way here," said Mish with a mischievous smile.

Kess gripped the flashlight. "Are you sure you don't have a knife or something?" A thought occurred to her. "Wait here."

Kess jogged to the back of the foyer and peered around the corner into the kitchen. It looked like a canteen, with seating in the front and ovens and benches behind a serving area. She ducked into the kitchen area and searched around. She soon found what she was after. She cantered back to where Mish was waiting. It was only then she realized she had left the other woman alone, in the dark, and weaponless. "Sorry," she said at the look on Mish's face. "But I found this." Kess waved a carving knife.

"Good grief."

"Better safe than murdered."

"Are you coming?" David's voice echoed up to them.

"Yes!" Mish bellowed back. "Just a minute." She put a hand on Kess's arm. "Just don't stab anyone by accident, ok?"

"Sure." Kess passed the flashlight to Mish, who pointed it towards the stairs. They crept across the foyer to the top of the stairs and peered down. The staircase wound its way into the dark. Mish's eyes gleamed in the half light. She was practically hopping with anticipation.

Kess bit her lip. "Do you know something, about what's down there?"

"I thought if I told you, you probably wouldn't come."

"Told me what?" Kess shone the torch directly at Mish, who covered her eyes from the glare.

"Careful with that."

"Tell me!"

"Fine!"

Kess lowered the flashlight, and shone it down the stairs once more. "What's down there?"

"I'm assuming it's the basement. I never went down there, last time. Lost my nerve. So this place has been closed for years. But as you can see, it's not exactly locked up. A few weeks ago, they found a body down there."

"What? Wait, is this a crime scene?" Exactly how many people had died at Willow Close over the years? Kess shivered.

"No, it was natural causes. Not a mark on him, apparently. He was some homeless kid who had been living in here, and he had a heart attack."

"And the reason you didn't want to tell me is?"

"It's nothing really. Just, they said he had been doing rituals down there. Satanic stuff."

"And?"

"That rumor about the teachers who were punishing the students? Part of it was that they were conducting some sort of ancient ritual. There were accusations of satanism."

"You think it's connected?"

"I think that place is where it all started."

Kess shivered again. In her bones, she knew Mish was right. The basement of Willow Close; that was where everything had begun.

"Should I come back up?" David's voice echoed up the stairs again.

"No. We're coming now!" yelled Mish. She looked at Kess. "Now or never."

Mish took Kess's free hand, and the pair made their way down the stairs towards the basement. Their footsteps echoed in the cold dark.

5

Mrs Henderson sat the tray on the coffee table with a clatter. A pitcher of lemonade and two faded, floral-patterned tumbler glasses rocked precariously. Ice shifted and cracked in the jug. "Lemonade, dear?"

"Yes, thank you." Kess leaned forward and retrieved a tumbler. She tipped it to her lips and let the sour liquid cascade down her throat. The tartness reached out and slapped her, but she welcomed its touch. Her brain was all kinds of fuzzy this morning, and it'd taken her ages to find where she'd parked her car. She was hoping the cold acid of the beverage would help wake her up.

"I hope you don't mind me saying this, dear, but you look tired. Is everything alright?"

Kess rubbed her eyes. "Fine. I just didn't sleep well." The truth was, she didn't remember how or when she had slept. She had woken this morning with a ball of calico fur curled on her chest, light streaming in the windows, and no recollection of coming home the previous night. Had she been drinking? That seemed unlikely. Yet her throat was raw and her head ached.

Mrs Henderson tutted kindly. "You young things."

Kess had been trying all morning to focus on instructing Mrs Henderson on the computer. The nephew had been worse than useless, as expected. The woman barely had any grip on the basics. But Kess felt so vague she had barely muddled through her usual tutorials. Finally, Mrs Henderson had ushered her into the living room and disappeared to get the tray. Kess felt bad. She should probably promise to come back again soon, to make up for her poor performance.

"Eat a cookie, dear. It will make you feel better." Mrs Henderson gestured to a plate of sugar cookies. Kess picked one up and nibbled the edges. She was right. The sugar did help. But what on earth had happened last night? She remembered standing in the foyer of Willow Close. The metal door behind the stairs. They had walked down those stairs, she was sure. Yet she had no memory of anything that had come after.

A huge fluff of grey fur wound around her legs. "Hello, Finnegan." Kess bent to pat the cat, and a chainsaw purr leapt to life, rumbling around the living room.

"He remembers you," beamed Mrs Henderson, sipping her lemonade. "Eat another cookie, dear, it's Binty's old family recipe."

"Binty from Bridge? Where do you all play?"

"Down at the yacht club, dear. It's only a few streets from here."

Kess's phone beeped. She retrieved it from her bag, which was slung on the floor near the chair. It was Mish. "Do you mind if I take this?"

She glanced at Mrs Henderson, who shook her head. "Go ahead, dear. I need to go and make the rounds, anyway." She pried herself off the chair and waved at Finnegan. "Lunch time, my boy. Let's find your siblings, shall we?"

Kess swiped the phone and Mish's voice blared into her ear. "Where are you!?"

"What do you mean? I'm…at a client's place. Working."

"Are you ok?"

"I think so." Kess scratched the hair under her ponytail. "About last night…"

"What do you remember?" Mish's voice was strained, frantic. It made her heart thump.

"We were standing in the foyer. Then we went down the stairs, I think. My memory sort of cuts out after that. Did we go to a bar or something after? Was I drinking?"

"No… No. You don't remember?"

"Remember what? Mish, what happened last night?" Kess gripped her phone, knuckles turning white.

"At the bottom of the stairs was this…place. I don't know. I mean, it was the basement, as we were expecting. But it looked like a dungeon or something. It felt like it was definitely used for punishment. There were curtains on the walls and some sort of weird circle with symbols on the floor. Remember what I said before, about the place getting closed down? The rumors? Mistreatment of children? Satanic rituals? I think it was all true, and that's where it happened." Symbols. Rituals. Kess thought back to their conversation at the top of the stairs.

"The place was really creepy. But that's not even… I mean, there was this wardrobe."

"What are you talking about? A wardrobe? If this is some half-assed joke about Narnia…"

"Just listen! The wardrobe had these big scratches on it, like something tore its way out. There were chains on the ground. I think maybe the whole thing had been chained up. But not anymore. I think that man, the one who died, let something out."

"Mish…"

"Listen. When we got in front of the wardrobe, both you and David started to act really weird. Holding hands and muttering these phrases to each other. It was really scary. In the end, I dragged you back out to the car. Brought you home. Your address was on your license and your keys were in your bag. You calmed down and went straight to sleep." There was a long pause, cut by the rattle of ice cubes. It was mid-morning, but it sounded like Mish was drinking. The edges of her words were slurred. "Are you sure you don't remember any of this?"

"No." Kess's heart was pounding. "What about David?"

"We left him there."

"We just…left him?"

"I couldn't carry both of you. Can you meet me later? We'd better go to the school."

"Sure."

"Are you ok? Really ok?"

"I think so. Mish, what phrases? What were we saying?

"I couldn't really understand. But something about…a deer and a dark place?" Cold tendrils shivered down Kess's spine. The fawn. The dark place.

Mish rang off and Kess sank back into her chair. She felt cold all over. She picked up her glass, and drained the lemonade in one acidic swallow. It didn't help.

Mrs Henderson flustered back into the room. "I can't find them, the silly girls. I suppose they'll be back when they're hungry." She moved about the room, dusting with a dish towel.

"I should get going," said Kess. "I'm sorry I wasn't much help today. Can I come back next week, perhaps?"

"That would be lovely, dear." Mrs Henderson beamed in a way that made Kess think she was more appreciative of the company than the computer support. "Take care out there. He's reached the outskirts, you know. New Haven."

"Who has?" With a sinking feeling in her stomach, Kess already knew who Mrs Henderson meant.

"The Family Man."

Kess frowned. There were pieces of the puzzle she didn't yet understand. Perhaps it would help if she knew more. "Mrs Henderson, how does he kill the families, do you know?"

"Oh yes. It's quite the topic at bridge. He always kills them in exactly the same way. One of adults has their head drilled, one has their legs and wrists slashed. For the children, one is clubbed to death, unrecognizable. And he always leaves one sitting in a chair."

"In a chair?"

"With their eyes taped open, like they're being forced to watch."

"Alive?"

"No, dear. None of them are ever left alive."

Kess's mind turned cartwheels. In the recesses of her memory, a hand with bloody knuckles reached out to open a rusty gate. A whitewashed house. Sad, dilapidated. With worn carpets. Oil that dripped on the walls and soaked the floor. Somewhere, in the background, a drill that whirred and a knife that made a *snick, snick, snick*, sound across delicate flesh. Why were these images in her mind? Why did she already know how the Family Man killed his victims?

Kess's phone pinged. In a trance, she picked it up and checked. She assumed it was Mish, sending details of their meeting this afternoon. But it was a Discord alert. Someone had played her game. She had forgotten she'd even posted it. Why on earth had she been driven to create a game called *Save the Fawn*? They'd been muttering about a deer, she and David. What had he said, that day in the classroom: *He always kills the deer?* Who was David talking about? Who or what was the fawn?

Kess clicked the alert. Someone had posted a message in reply to her game and when she opened Discord there was also an image. The message read: "No one can save the fawn. Not even you." With a sinking feeling, Kess stared at the picture. It showed a blackboard, with uneven letters scrawled in a red that dripped like blood: *See you in the Dark Place.*

Kess dropped her phone back into her bag, fingers shaking. Her heart was beating fast. Sweat ran down her neck and her hands were cold.

"Is everything alright, dear?" Mrs Henderson had stopped fussing around the room and was watching Kess.

"Fine," Kess lied, getting to her feet and rubbing her hands on her jeans. "I'd better get home."

There was a sudden wail from the back yard. The sound of cats fighting. Hisses and screams.

"Fiona! Felicity!" Yelled Mrs Henderson, hurtling out of the room in the direction of the yard. "Felix!" After a moment, there was a din of banging saucepans and Mrs Henderson yelling.

Kess hovered, wondering whether to go and see what was happening. She was still shaking from the message on her phone. She wanted to go home and sleep, forget about all of it. As she stood undecided, a pile of grey fur hurtled past and disappeared under the dining table. Finnegan. She knelt down.

His eyes looked wild and his hair was matted and wet. Kess reached out a hand. "It's ok." But Finnegan flattened his tufted ears hard against his skull and swiped a paw at her, claws extended. A dull wail came from his throat. Kess bent down further, trying to see if he was injured. There was a trail of red in the carpet where he had pressed himself down to crawl under the table. The light was weak under the table, but it looked like his fur was matted with red. Blood? Had he been fighting with the other cats?

Kess straightened up, unsure what to do. She was too tired for any of this, but she should probably ask Mrs Henderson. Check the other cats were ok. Everything seemed suddenly quiet. The saucepans had stopped banging. The cats had stopped wailing. Mrs Henderson had stopped yelling.

Kess took a breath, and walked firmly towards the kitchen. "Mrs Henderson?" she called. She hadn't been through to the kitchen before. But she knew it was just beyond the living room. There was an uneasy feeling in her stomach, twisting and turning. Why was it so quiet?

She walked through the doorway, and with relief, saw Mrs Henderson. The woman was facing out the open patio door, looking across the yard. It was definitely the back yard from the photos. The swing set sat in a corner on the grass. The colors had faded over time, but it was the same set. There were fuzzy cushions on each seat. The white-iron furniture sat, paint peeling and flaking, on the patio. One of the chairs was overturned. There were no cats in sight.

"What happened?" Kess moved towards Mrs Henderson. The woman seemed to be leaning against the countertop next to the door, peering intently into the yard. "Did you find Felix, and Felicity, and… Fiona?"

Kess reached out a hand and placed it on Mrs Henderson's shoulder. She half-expected the woman to jump in surprise, but she made no move. There was no sign she even knew Kess was there. "Mrs Henderson, are you alright?" Kess pulled gently on her shoulder, turning her around.

Mrs Henderson's eyes were glazed and unseeing. From the center of her forehead protruded a dark handle studded with steel. The sort generally attached to a bowie knife. Kess stared. The knife blade was buried deep in Mrs Henderson's head. Blood oozed and dripped from the wound, staining her dress.

Dislodged from her stable position against the counter, Mrs Henderson slowly toppled sideways. She fell to the floor with a thud and lay unmoving, blood pooling around her on the kitchen tiles. The knife stuck straight out of her head, buried, as it was, right up to the hilt.

Kess was not a screamer. The shock shuddered through her in terrifying silence. She covered her mouth with her hands and stared. Her heart galloped and nausea roiled. She felt fixed to the spot. Stuck in slow-motion.

There was a noise at the back of the garden. Kess looked up. A figure in a dark hood was watching. For some reason, she thought immediately of the figure she had seen briefly in the rear-view mirror near the old chemical plant. Her heart stuttered. She still couldn't see the face. It was like a black hole. But the frame was big and bulky. Struggling to fit within its clothes. Things rippled beneath the surface. Muscles and tendons too overgrown to fit within the skin and pinpoints hinting at rows of spines lurking just beneath the surface.

Time lurched forward in slow motion. Kess noticed several things at once. First, the cushions on the swings were not cushions. They were cats. Two of Mrs Henderson's cats had been posed on the swings, like fuzzy children, watching. Was that the last thing she had seen before she died? Blood was spattered across the patio. Chunks of fur littered the tiles and streaks of gore marred the faded white of the wrought-iron table. Kess felt a wave of nausea. Who would do something so horrible? This led to the second thing. The man in the hood held a knife in his hand. Lethal-looking steel with a dark handle. The same as the knife protruding from Mrs Henderson. Kess was face to face with the murderer. In her heart, she knew this hooded figure was the Family Man. Somehow, he was connected to her. Somehow, he had found her. Somehow, he had come for her.

She bit down on her lip. The pain helped focus her mind. The figure in the hood could close the distance between them in seconds. Slash her to pieces before she could even scream. How fast could she run? Not fast enough. Yet she had to run.

In one fluid movement, Kess hauled the patio door closed and lunged away, back towards the living room. She could feel the figure behind her, giving chase. She bolted through the living room, grabbing her bag from the floor. Then she ducked around the corner, into the bathroom, and slammed the door closed. She dropped the bag and grabbed the lock in both hands. Her fingers were shaking so badly she could barely grip it. With an effort, she drew the small bolt home. She hoped it would hold. The monster in the garden had looked strong enough to break the whole door down.

Her heart pounded. It had taken mere seconds to go from kitchen to bathroom. Her legs screamed with the effort. There was silence in the house beyond the bathroom door. No sound of anyone chasing. No crashing doors. No footsteps. Nothing. Heart in her mouth, Kess bent down and grabbed her phone from her bag. Her whole body shaking, she dialed the police. Then she sank onto the cool bathroom tiles, hands curled around her knees, and waited.

Eventually, somewhere in the distance, sirens wailed.

6

Mish burst into Mrs Henderson's small living room, candy-pink purse waving wildly. "Where is she?"

A forensic officer pointed to the sofa, where Kess sat, staring vacantly at the pastel wallpaper above the switched-off television. Mish flung herself onto the sofa, next to Kess, and wrapped an arm around her. "Are you alright? Stupid question, I know. But even so, are you?" Her voice was strained. "Is there anyone I should call?"

Kess's eyes traced the floral motif in the wallpaper. She supposed that was Mish's polite way of asking why, of all the people she presumably knew, Mish had been her first choice. How could she explain that she couldn't face the intrusion of her foster family, their cloying kindness? She didn't have the strength for them, not yet. Besides, they would want to take her back to Boston. She needed to stay. She had to figure out what was happening.

"I'm fine," Kess lied. "I just wondered if you could drive me home. I'm not sure if I should…"

"Of course, of course," Mish shushed her. "You absolutely shouldn't drive."

Forensic officers were moving back and forth, from the door to the living room and through to the kitchen. There were voices in the kitchen—police officers and perhaps the pathologist. Kess didn't want to think about it. The officers had coaxed her out of the bathroom and onto the sofa, saying she needed to wait in the house until they took her statement. After that, she could go home.

She cleared her throat. "If you're wondering why I didn't call someone else, it's because I don't really have anyone. But also, I called you because we need to talk." Kess lowered her voice to a whisper. "I saw him."

Mish leaned to speak into her ear. "The Family Man?"

Kess nodded, and Mish's eyes went wide. Before she could say more, a man in a business suit hustled into the living room from the direction of the kitchen. He held a cat carrier. A mild-mannered miaow came from within.

"You're the nephew," said Kess, eyeing him up and down. She knew him instantly, from the photograph on the mantelpiece and the smug attitude.

"Alistair Worthington." He gave a small head nod, setting the cat carrier down on the floor and rummaging in his wallet. He produced a business card, and handed it over. Kess ran her fingers over the glossy print. "Financial advisor. Really?" Holly would eat this guy for breakfast.

"You were a friend of my aunt?" She watched his eyes flick around the room and land on the empty lemonade tumblers. Mrs Henderson would never make that sweet, sour liquid again. Something pinched in Kess's chest. She bit her lip, hard.

"I helped set up the computer. My name's Kess. Kess Hawkins?"

"Oh right. Yes, I remember the name from the invoice. Pity she's not going to get much use out of it now." He looked vaguely annoyed at the inconvenience. That his aunt had died before getting his money's worth out of the new computer.

"I can take it back and do a full refund if you like."

"Would you? That's very generous. Thank you."

Kess nodded, glumly. "Of course."

"She was insistent that we get you. To do the computer. Now I can see why." The miaow from the cat carrier increased as he spoke. The carrier was rocking slightly as its inhabitant became more agitated.

"Where are you taking her cats?"

Alistair scratched his eyebrow. "I'm taking this one for my wife. She keeps nagging me to get a cat for our daughter. Seems well-behaved enough." The carrier lurched and he put out a foot to steady it. "Just a bit worked up. Doesn't seem to like the cage."

"Only the one?" Kess pried herself off the couch and crouched down in front of the cat carrier. A small grey tabby stared out, balefully. "Which one is this, do you know?

"It's one of the females, I don't know which. We'll rename it anyway. I mean, what sort of a name is Fiona or…"

"Felicity. Which I think means happy or lucky—like Felix." Except Felix hadn't been lucky at all. Kess peered closer. Blood dripped from the tabby-cat's mouth and chin. "Is she hurt?"

"No. It's not her blood." He tugged awkwardly at his collar. "The police found her beside my aunt."

Kess frowned. The tabby licked blood from her lips. Did he mean that they had found this cat eating Mrs Henderson? She shuddered.

Kess had been locked in the bathroom until the police arrived. She hadn't been allowed back into the kitchen—not that she would have wanted to watch the proceedings. Now she was doubly glad. She wouldn't have wanted see this little cat devouring the spilled blood from the floor, or worse. Kess straightened up, trying not to think about the small grey cat lapping at Mrs Henderson's blood. Alistair shifted uncomfortably.

"What about Finnegan?" Kess asked.

"Is that the big, angry one?"

"Yep." That seemed a pretty apt description of Finnegan.

"The wife wants a nice, pretty cat, not a huge, deranged monster."

Kess wound her hair around her fingers. As far as she knew, Finnegan was still hiding under the dining table. Of the two cats still alive, he was the one who hadn't been munching on his owner. "I could take him." The words were out of her mouth before she could think about it.

Alistair smiled superciliously. "You are being a really good sport about all this, you know."

Kess resisted the urge to punch him. "Is there another cat carrier?"

"She had one for each of them." Alistair turned on his expensively-shod heel and went to look for it.

Kess returned to the sofa, where Mish was frowning after the departing man. "What a douche."

"Totally." Kess tugged at her hair. "So now I have another computer and another cat."

"You already have a cat?"

"Gremlin. I have no idea how she's going to get along with Finnegan."

"You don't have to take him."

"I'm not leaving him. That asshole would probably have him euthanized."

Mish didn't reply. She probably knew Kess was right. Kess breathed, trying to calm her thoughts and think. "Do you mind coming to my place, to help get him settled? It'll be easier to talk there anyway."

"Of course I will. You shouldn't be alone."

"I'm fine." Kess watched the forensic officers moving back and forth. They were dusting the room for prints, even though the hooded figure hadn't been inside, as far as she knew. What if he had been standing out here silently, waiting and watching while she was hiding in the bathroom? Somehow that felt even worse than if he'd been trying to break the door down. She shivered and rubbed her arms.

The nephew re-emerged from the kitchen with a cat carrier, which he placed next to the sofa. "Good luck with him. And thanks again, about the computer."

"Sure." Kess narrowed her eyes. He didn't seem all that concerned about his aunt. Then she remembered the photographs on the mantelpiece. "What about her children?"

"Whose?"

"Your Aunt. Mrs Henderson. Do her actual children live nearby? Would they want…"

"She didn't have any kids." The nephew looked confused. "Just the cats."

"I mean, I'm sure they're grown up now but…"

"She never had any children." He frowned. "Did she say that she did? Maybe the old girl really was starting to lose it."

"The photos," said Kess, bewildered, "on the mantelpiece?"

"Probably some of her charges from that care home she worked at. She was always bringing home strays. Back in the '80s, no one kept much track of that stuff."

Kess blinked. While she was organizing her thoughts, Mish leaned forward, eyes glued to the nephew. "Which care home did she work at?"

The nephew wrinkled his nose. "That big ugly eyesore out of town. What was the name…. Willow Hill? Willow House?" Kess and Mish looked at each other.

"Willow Close," said Kess.

"We know it," said Mish.

As the nephew departed with his cat, a police officer emerged from the kitchen to take Kess's statement. Kess went back through everything that had happened since she had arrived at Mrs Henderson's house that morning. When she tried to describe the figure in the yard, the officer got very intense about the details.

"Could you come in to the station to look through some photos?"

"Sure, but I doubt it will help. With the hood, and the way the light was in the yard, I honestly couldn't see much of his face." Her hands were cold and clammy, and she was starting to feel vague and disconnected.

The officer closed his notebook. "But you're sure it was a man?"

Kess nodded. Though she hadn't seen the face, the frame had been that of a man—a muscled man. Limbs thick as trees. Something had been wrong about him, as though more than muscles lurked beneath the shirt. Growths and tendons and spines. Like he was more than a man. He was a predator. A hunter. She started shivering all over.

"And did you see the murder weapon?"

"The knife…in Mrs Henderson's head?"

"It was removed from the scene. We assume by the killer."

Kess got a nasty flash in her mind, of the hunter ripping the knife free from Mrs Henderson's motionless form. Of him licking the blood from the blade. The officer was looking at her, expectantly. She tried to wrangle herself under control. "It was…silver with a black handle. A hunting knife, I guess. The same as the one he was holding."

"Nylon, wood, or bone?"

"What?" She clasped her hands together to stop them shaking.

"The handle."

"It was…shiny?" How would she know what it was made of? Kess had never had much to do with hunting knives. And she hadn't had a chance to look closely. She hadn't exactly lingered in the kitchen. She felt a wash of anger. Then a wave of loss. Her emotions were shifting so fast her head was spinning.

The officer scribbled in his notebook. "After we take your prints, you can go home. Don't leave town. We will likely have more questions."

Mish piped up from her spot on the sofa. "Do you have any theories, why someone would do this?"

"Probably a robbery." The officer answered curtly. Mish darted a look at Kess. The officer knew as well as they did that nothing had been taken. Then there was the matter of the cats, posed deliberately on the swings. Robbers didn't usually do that sort of thing. That was serial killer territory.

Kess put a hand on Mish's arm. "I just want to go home."

The officer went to fetch the fingerprint taker. After Kess had given a set of prints and a DNA swab, she was released. "Keep an eye on her tonight," the officer said to Mish. "She's probably in shock. Keep her warm and make sure she gets something to eat." Mish nodded and promised to look after her.

It took the concerted efforts of both Kess and Mish to coax Finnegan into a cat carrier. He swooshed his tail and wailed at them, but they finally persuaded him inside. He could have put up more of a fight if he'd wanted, Kess thought. His protests were mostly for show. She had a feeling Finnegan knew about Mrs Henderson, and didn't fancy his chances with the nephew any more than she had.

Before she left, Kess walked over to the mantelpiece and looked once more at Mrs Henderson's photos. She picked up the one with the children on the swing set and wiped the dust from the glass. Peering into it close up, she could see the children's faces more clearly. They were in the background of the shot, but even so, they looked like the children in Mish's photo. It looked like a photo of her and David, sitting on the swing set in Mrs Henderson's back yard. How was that possible?

After all that had happened, her mind could easily be playing tricks on her. It *must* be playing tricks. She had never even met Mrs Henderson before being asked to set up the computer. It had been a very long day. She probably needed to sleep. She replaced the photo and followed Mish out of the house. She couldn't shake the uneasy feeling that things were spiraling out of control, unravelling. That somehow her whole life, everything she took for granted, was a lie.

It was only after they got into Mish's car, with a computer and a wailing cat on the back seat, headed in the direction of Kess's place, that she remembered they had been supposed to go to the school. "What about David?" she murmured. Her eyes were refusing to stay open. Her whole body was suddenly aching for sleep.

"After we talked before, I phoned the school and pretended to be a parent. He picked up the line and I hung up. So, we know he made it back."

"And we know he was in school this morning," Kess muttered. The school was not far from Mrs Henderson's house. They would need to check exactly when David Collier had been in class to rule him out.

"You don't think it was him you saw in the yard?"

"I don't think so. But I can't be sure."

Mish was silent. Kess pried her eyes open and looked at her. She was shifting her eyes back and forth, clearly uncomfortable. There was something she wasn't saying.

"What is it?"

"Now is really not the time." Mish flicked an indicator and changed lanes, edging towards the harbor.

"Just tell me." Kess felt like she couldn't take much more, but she needed to know everything. There were too many secrets already. She braced herself.

"Kess, I think David Collier is your brother."

7

Gremlin peered nervously from her perch on top of the fridge. Finnegan glowered up from his position under the kitchen table. His long, thick tail swooshed to and fro.

"He's not going to eat your cat, is he?"

"I hope not." Kess and Mish were leaning against the bench, watching the cats get acquainted. Kess had opened a bottle of white wine that she and Mish had already made significant progress demolishing. It had been a very long day. "I think, under all that fur, he's actually a big softie."

"Let's hope you're right." Mish looked skeptical. Kess sympathized with Finnegan. She often made a bad first impression on people too.

"Did you want something to eat? There's…pizza rolls and…to be honest, probably not much else."

Mish narrowed her eyes. "How old are you?" She strode over and opened the fridge. She stuck her head right in, inspecting the contents. "Good grief, are you serious?" She withdrew her head and gave Kess a withering look. "Have you ever even met a vegetable?"

Kess snorted. "Sorry, what do you have in your fridge?"

"Actual food." Mish had already given a less than glowing assessment of the apartment—though, to be fair, "retro '80s infused nerd-wonderland" sounded absolutely fine to Kess. As did not eating vegetables. "We'll have to order something," Mish said, clacking her fingernails on the Formica.

"The take-out menu box is over there." Kess pointed to a small cardboard box, which had once housed a graphics card. It was now stuffed to bursting with menus from every take-out place within delivery distance.

"Don't you just use your phone?"

"I'm old school. I like to peruse my options."

Mish was shaking her head, like she'd stumbled through the looking glass. Meanwhile, Gremlin had hopped down from the fridge to the bench and was sniffing in the direction of Finnegan. His tail was still waving, but he looked like he was tolerating the attention. "Good kitties," said Kess, moving between them and giving them head scratches.

"I guess we can try the pizza rolls?" Mish sounded beaten. She had prodded listlessly through the take-out box, but it seemed the wealth of paper menus had defeated her.

"Yep." Kess moved to the freezer, grabbed a new box of pizza rolls and cracked them open. She shoved them onto the tray and into the oven, flicking on the timer in one smooth movement.

"You look like you do that a lot."

Kess shrugged. She chugged the rest of her glass of wine, and then grabbed a soda. Moving around the bench, she made her way to the sofa and collapsed onto it. Mish topped up her own glass with wine, then followed and perched on one of the armchairs.

"Time to talk?"

Kess nodded. She was so tired, she felt like her brain might explode. "You think David's my brother?" They hadn't mentioned it since the car. She'd needed to get the cats sorted out, and imbibe some alcohol, before giving the matter her full attention.

Mish combed her fingers through her hair. She looked nervous. "The thing is, I ran a DNA test."

That jolted Kess awake, despite herself. "Excuse me?"

"Last night, in the basement of the orphanage, when you two were muttering, which by the way was really scary—thanks for that. I just started thinking. Or, I guess I had this gut feeling. I thought, what if you were related? So…I took a saliva sample, from both of you."

Kess didn't know whether to be angry or impressed. In the terror of the basement, with two basically catatonic people, Mish had had the presence of mind to get a saliva sample?

"You just happened to have some swabs on you?"

"For emergency journalistic research purposes, yeah."

Kess frowned. There was clearly a lot to unpack there. But given the situation she'd have to let the details and ethics slide, she was way too interested in the results. "The samples were a match?"

"Familial match. It's not absolute, I guess. But chances are, he's your brother."

Kess scratched her head. "I mean, it's possible, I guess. But I have no memory of having a brother. So, I guess I never knew him?" An image of a car filled with water came into her mind. She had dreamed she was floating in water, next to a boy. Could that boy have been David?

"You were raised in care, possibly at the orphanage for a time. Maybe you were separated?" Mish looked as doubtful as Kess felt. The whole situation was surreal.

A deep, rumbling purr echoed from the direction of the kitchen. Kess hopped up to look. In the middle of the kitchen floor sat Gremlin and Finnegan. Finnegan had a paw draped casually over Gremlin's head, and the little cat was busily licking his fur. As Kess watched, Finnegan leaned forward and licked Gremlin's face, almost knocking her over. She wobbled, then resumed licking him. It seemed as though the pair were going to get along just fine. Relief cascaded through her. At least that was one problem solved.

"That is adorable." Mish was leaning over the back of the chair, peering into the kitchen. "Almost makes me want a pet."

"You don't have any?"

"I had a fish for a while." The dubious tone made Kess think that the situation had not ended well for the fish. Not everyone was born to be a pet owner.

She gave the cats some food while she was waiting for the oven to finish. When the timer dinged, she used an oven mitt to retrieve the pizza rolls, and soon she and Mish were sitting in the living room with plates balanced on their laps.

"These are not as bad as I expected," said Mish when she had devoured her first roll.

"I basically live on them," said Kess, with no shame.

"You don't entertain a lot, huh?"

"My social life is over there." Kess nodded at the computer.

"Girl, I need to take you out on the town sometime."

"I'm ok." Kess wondered what it would be like to party with someone like Mish. She had never really been into the social scene. But Mish's parents were rich, she had probably been dragged from glamorous function to function since childhood. Country clubs, yacht clubs…

"Binty and Bridge!" said Kess suddenly.

"What?" Mish almost choked on her pizza roll.

"Mrs Henderson plays—played—bridge with a bunch of ladies over in West Haven, at the yacht club near her house. What if some of them used to work with her, at Willow Close?"

"We could get some more information about its history." Mish's eyes were gleaming. "That is an excellent idea."

Kess smiled. As she went to bite into another pizza roll, Finnegan gave a low wail from the kitchen, and Gremlin hissed. The hair on the back of her neck stood up. "Kitties," she said warningly, putting her plate down and getting up to check on them. But the cats weren't fighting, they were both staring at the window near the kitchen table. Kess's heart thudded. What was worrying them? Slowly, she walked across the room. The small window looked out towards the water. She had placed the table there for that reason. Shimmying behind the table, Kess pushed the curtains aside, placed her hands on the windowsill, and looked out.

Moonlight reflected from the water. Boats moved lazily at their moorings. All seemed peaceful. She squinted. At the harbor's edge a figure was standing, looking up towards the window. A hooded figure.

A hand reached out and touched her shoulder. Kess jumped and let out a squeak. But it was only Mish. The woman had come into the kitchen to see why she was taking so long. The kitties were still rumbling their disapproval, tails swishing.

"Don't sneak up on me." Kess turned to glare at Mish, who held up her hands.

"Sorry. What did you see out there?"

Kess turned back to the window, but the figure was gone. "I thought I saw someone. A man in a hood."

"The Family Man?" Mish's eyes went wide.

"I don't know. Maybe. Or maybe just some regular person in a hood."

Mish nudged her aside and stared out the window. "I don't see anyone."

Kess crossed the apartment and checked that the door was locked. Her heart was thumping, and she felt jittery and wired. "It's been a long day. I could have imagined it."

Mish walked over to the door and double-checked the locks. "Perhaps. But just in case, do you have something heavy we could move in front of this door?"

"One of the armchairs, maybe?"

Together, they wrestled an armchair down the short hallway and lodged it in front of the door, jamming the handle.

"Better," said Mish appraisingly. "What about windows?"

"Unless he's a climber, the windows would be difficult." Kess checked the locks on the kitchen window and living room sliding doors. There was a small balcony outside the living room, but it was two stories up with nothing to either side, and in full view of the other buildings.

Mish gave her a look, and of one mind, they picked up her white-wood dining table and placed it in front of the living room balcony doors. Then they sat, Kess flopped on the sofa and Mish draped more elegantly in the remaining armchair.

"What now?" Kess batted Gremlin away from the coffee table, where she was trying to snag Mish's last unfinished pizza roll. Finnegan sauntered in and squeezed himself under the table. After a moment, Gremlin ducked under the table and curled up next to him. At least the kitties were getting along.

"Tomorrow, we definitely need to talk to David, and check out these bridge-playing, yacht-club ladies. As for right now, I don't know. We wait?"

As she said that, there was a knock at the door. A quick, decisive, *tap tap tap.*

Kess sat bolt upright. Mish half-stood, but resumed her seat with a thump. "What do we do?"

"It could be anyone. Do I answer it?"

They looked at each other. Kess got up, then sat down again. The kitties peeped in turns from under the coffee table, curious about all the commotion. As they dithered, the knock came again, louder and more insistent. *Tap, tap, tap.*

"Ignore it?" said Mish, her voice wavering and unsure.

"The lights are on, whoever it is can already see someone's home."

Kess stood up. Mish rose, and closed the distance between them to grip Kess's arm. Her hands were like ice. The knock came again, this time very loud and with enough force to shake the door frame. *Bang, bang, bang!*

Kess tiptoed to the door, with Mish following, still clutching her arm. She paused in the hallway, swallowed hard, and in a trembling voice called: "Who is it?"

There was silence on the other side of the door. Then the knock came again, making them both jump. *Bang, bang, bang!*

"Who is it?" called Kess again. This time she tried to make her voice sound authoritative, but it wobbled far more than she wanted.

Again, there was no answer. Kess looked at Mish, who shrugged. She was trying to look calm, but her eyes were wild and her fingernails were still digging into the flesh of Kess's arm. The doorknob started to rattle. Kess and Mish jumped backwards. The doorknob rattled, more and more furiously. Then the knocking came again, loud and insistent. *Bang, bang, bang!*

Mish took a small step forward. "We're calling the police!" she yelled at full volume. Then she grabbed Kess, and dragged her back to the living room. Mish fished in her bag, grabbed her phone, and started dialing. There was silence from the other side of the door. Kess couldn't take her eyes off it. The door seemed to loom and grow and move towards her. Who, or what, was out there?

A scrabbling, scratching sound came from the other side of the door. Something was searching and seeking for a way in. Mish was talking loudly on the phone. Her voice was as panicked as Kess felt.

Mish hung up as the scratching noises stopped. "I called my friend. He's in the police. Or he used to be, long story. He can protect us. He's on his way now."

"How far away does he live?"

"Actually, he was already driving downtown, so he's close. Five minutes? Ten?"

"What do we do until then?"

"Whoever, whatever is out there, I don't think it can get in." Mish's eyes darted around the apartment, looking for other entry points. Kess looked around too. This place had always felt so safe, but now she was having to think of all the ways it might not be. She shivered. Cold fingers walked up and down her spine. Suddenly, she felt like she might cry. So much had transpired. Willow Close. Mrs Henderson and her cats. Now this. She was cold and exhausted. Why was all this happening? Mish hugged her. "It will be alright." Kess wrapped her arms around Mish. They stood in the living room, clutching each other, eyes glued on the door. All was silence.

After perhaps ten minutes, there was a sharp rap on the door. Both jumped, and Mish squealed. Then a deep male voice called: "Michelle? Are you in there? This is Travis."

"Travis!" Mish lunged towards the door. Kess followed. They moved the chair and opened the door, barely enough for Travis to squeeze in. Kess stuck her head into the corridor to look around. It was empty. They moved the chair back into place behind the doorknob.

"Did you see anyone out there?" Mish towed Travis into the living room.

"No one."

Kess followed them back into the living room. Travis turned to her. "You're Kess, I presume. I'm Travis." He stuck out a hand and she shook it. Travis was exceedingly good looking—a tall, black man who looked about thirty-ish and was absolutely shredded. Muscles bulged under his designer t-shirt. A light jacket was slung over his shoulder, complementing fashionably ripped black jeans and trainers. His look was expensively casual, Kess thought. He was probably every bit as much at home with the country club set as Mish. Was that how they had met?

When Travis sat in the armchair, Mish perched on its arm. He stroked her back. "Sounds like you've had quite a night."

Mish gave Travis a rundown of everything that had happened, while Kess sat on the sofa. Gremlin hopped up into her lap, and as she stroked the soft fur, she started feeling slightly better.

"There was nobody out there. I had a quick look around as I came in." Travis seemed calm and decisive. She could see the trace of police efficiency, though Mish had said he wasn't in the force anymore.

She cleared her throat. "Mish said you used to be a cop?"

"Yeah," Travis' mouth tightened. "I liked the job, but some of the people…"

"He's in private security now."

"And investigations."

"Like a private eye?" Kess imagined a clichéd detective-noir office, a Humphrey Bogart-style character holding a glass of whiskey, ice cubes clinking in the glass, a hard-boiled, cynical monologue narrating his experiences.

"Something like that," Travis grinned at her. His teeth were perfect. "So, not to be all private detective, but do you have any new leads?"

Kess flicked her eyes to Mish and raised an eyebrow, questioning how much to tell him.

"He already knows everything," Mish shrugged. "Who do you think ran the DNA sample for me?"

"I still have friends on the force, and down at the lab." Travis smoothed a strand of hair from Mish's face and gazed into her eyes. "I'm glad you both are alright."

"It was pretty scary," said Mish, gazing back at him. He planted a reassuring kiss on her forehead. Kess wondered how long the two had been dating. Mish obviously trusted him. He seemed solid enough. A good guy.

"We're going to follow up on some stuff tomorrow. But right now, I don't know."

"Think. Is there any other way you can find out who this guy is?"

Kess replayed the day in her mind. She didn't want to think about Mrs Henderson, but she forced herself to go back through the events. Her stomach jolted with surprise. How had she forgotten? *Her game!* "I think he sent me a message." Travis and Mish looked at her in surprise. Quickly, she explained about her game.

She showed them the message on the boards: "No one can save the fawn, not even you." And the picture, with blood scrawling down the blackboard: "See you in the Dark Place."

"Don't ask me to explain the message—I don't know if I can put it in words."

"But it definitely means something to you?"

"Yes."

"And you think it's from him?"

"I don't think there's anyone else it could be from." Kess's hands trembled. Gremlin sniffed her fingers, then started licking them.

Travis folded his arms, and stared into space, until Mish prodded his impressive triceps with a polished fingernail. "What are you thinking?"

"I'm thinking that maybe we can trace the message. Find out where this guy lives."

The three looked at each other. "Is that safe?" said Mish, voice wavering.

Travis put his arms around her and pulled her down into his lap. He rested his chin on her hair. "I'll protect you both."

Kess gritted her teeth. "I don't think we have a choice. We have to find the Family Man, whoever he is, before he finds us."

8

That night, Kess dreamed of Willow Close. The lawns and gardens were pristine. Manicured hedges studded with white flowers gave the air a sweet, floral fragrance. The walnut door stood wide open, welcoming. She was walking up the main stairs between the stone pillars. As she stepped from the sunshine onto the polished, black and white tiles of the entry foyer, it felt like coming home. The black walnut bannisters gleamed in the rays of sun falling through the open door, and the bright sound of children singing echoed from the room to the left of the hall. From her right, she could hear someone reciting mathematics tables. She could smell roasting chicken wafting down from the kitchen.

As Kess walked forward into the hall, an elegant woman swept down the staircase. "Ms Hawkins. We've been waiting for you."

"I was in the garden," said Kess dreamily. "The sunshine is so warm today."

"The fresh air is good for you, dear." The woman smiled as she reached Kess. She seemed familiar. As Kess's eyes adjusted to the change in light, she realized the woman was Mrs Henderson. She looked much younger. A mass of warm brown hair cascaded around her shoulders, and her eyes, though the same pale blue, seemed brighter. Not as clouded by age.

"Mrs Henderson?"

"Dora, dear. How many times do I need to tell you? It's absolutely fine to call me Dora. We're all family here."

A shiver ran down Kess's spine at the mention of the word 'family', but she brushed it off. "Yes Mrs...Dora."

Mrs Henderson beamed at her. "That's the way, dear." She put a hand on Kess's shoulder. "Now, would you like to go and get a cup of tea, or shall we get started? Leon and David are already here."

"Now is fine," Kess said. She couldn't quite remember why she was here, or what she had to do. Why was David here too? And who was Leon?

"Good girl." Mrs Henderson steered Kess towards the staircase, but instead of climbing the stairs, they walked around behind them. To the metal door in the wall. The door swung open with a well-oiled smoothness. The staircase beyond was lit with lamps. Slowly, they descended the stairs.

The basement of Willow Close was much nicer than she had expected. It was an oblong room, with velvet curtains draped around the perimeter. The floor was a gleaming black, like rich marble. Comfortable chairs sat at intervals around a large open central space. In the center of the floor a circle was drawn with strange symbols marked in a white powder, perhaps chalk. At the far end of the room, a huge mahogany wardrobe was pushed against the wall. It was a massive thing, ornately carved with figures jutting out from the woodwork. The figures looked like angels and devils and other mythological creatures. Kess had never seen anything like it, and yet part of her felt that she had seen this particular wardrobe many times before.

Teachers were clustered within the room. They stood or sat, some holdings glasses or china cups. They were smiling and chatting, as if they were standing in the canteen or classroom, not some strange room in the basement. Soft classical music played in the background. To the side, where Kess and Mrs Henderson stood, a long buffet table was crowded with little plates of food and tea, coffee and other beverages. Teachers came and went, gathering small plates of finger food and drinks. In the center of the table, in pride of place, a large crystal punchbowl sat, full of swirling red liquid.

"It really is just punch, dear." Kess flicked her eyes back to Mrs Henderson, who was smiling down at her. "But if you prefer, there's a jug of my homemade lemonade at the end. I think I've almost got the recipe right. It just needs a little more tartness. I can never quite get it sour enough." Her eyes twinkled. For some reason, Kess's own eyes filled with tears at the mention of Mrs Henderson's lemonade.

"There, there, dear. I know this is very strange, but believe me, it is necessary. Willow Close exists to protect not just you, but everyone." Mrs Henderson swept her hands out to indicate the world beyond the school.

"Protect them from what?" asked Kess, a nervous hitch in her voice.

"Evil, dear. The evil that lives in Willow Hill."

Mrs Henderson steered her towards the front of the room, where the wardrobe waited. Kess's heart thudded in her chest. What evil? What was she talking about? As they reached the wardrobe, two children stood from where they had been sitting against the wall. She recognized the boy from the photograph, David.

The other boy had strawberry-blonde hair and warm, brown eyes. She stared at him, curious, but he ignored her, looking instead at Mrs Henderson. "When can we play?"

"Soon, dear." She squeezed Kess's shoulder. "It's time now."

Two teachers stepped to the wardrobe and swung the doors open. Kess gasped. The back of the wardrobe had been removed, so that the wall beyond was clearly visible. Only it wasn't a wall, not exactly. A huge crack ran the length of the brick wall visible at the back of the wardrobe. Light and shadows moved within the crack.

"In you go, dears," said Mrs Henderson, giving Kess a firm push. She dug in her heels, but David and Leon took her by the hands and pulled her into the wardrobe to sit with them. They sat, cross-legged inside the wardrobe, staring at the crack in the wall. Behind them, a chant began. Kess knew, without turning, that the teachers had assembled behind them, standing at various points on the strange circle of dust. The chant rose, words that were unintelligible to her ears. They sounded mystical and old, imbued with ancient magic.

The crack in the wall shuddered. It seemed to pull and grow. David and Leon squeezed Kess's hands. Her heart was hammering. She could barely breathe. As she watched, the crack spilt open and tentacles reached out towards them. Along the length of the tendrils were suckers, with little mouths that opened and closed. Kess opened her mouth to scream, but no sound came out. To each side, she could see tentacles wrapping around David and Leon. She wanted to scream, to run, but she could not move. Eyes bulging and heart racing, Kess watched as the last tentacle, little mouths opening and closing, came towards her. With a sound like a soft kiss, the suckers attached to her skin. The mouths moved against her. She could feel them burrowing. But there was no pain.

Encapsulated, unable to move, the doors of the wardrobe closed behind them. The three children sat together in the dark. In front of them, the crack in the wall began to open. Soon, they could see beyond the wall. Into the dark place.

She woke with a start to find Mish shaking her by the shoulders. She was on her sofa, in her apartment. Travis hovered in the background.

She must have fallen asleep.

"Are you alright?" demanded Mish. "You were muttering in your sleep, and then you started shaking."

Kess eyed her. "I think his name was Leon."

"What?"

"The boy in the photograph. His name is Leon."

"Did you remember something? Willow Close?" Mish waved at Travis, "Get her some water."

Kess sat up and ran a hand through her hair. "I think you were right all along. I was there. But my memories have been changed somehow, or lost. I don't know."

"Did you see anything else?" Mish sat down on the arm of the sofa.

"David, and a wardrobe. It was huge, and carved with all sorts of…"

"Weird figures and things. Yeah, that's the one in the basement. What were they doing down there?"

"It was some kind of ritual. And Mrs Henderson was there."

Travis brought her a glass of water and she drained it in one go. "Thanks. What time is it?" The sun seemed to be creeping through the windows. The kitties were curled up together in a ball in Gremlin's cat bed. Neither seemed about to stir.

"Early. Just gone five. I hope you don't mind, but we crashed in your spare room after you fell asleep. You passed out pretty hard, we didn't want to wake you."

"That's fine. I hope the room wasn't too dusty." In Kess's mind, the dream still swirled and faded. She tried to grasp on to the details, but it kept slipping away. What had happened once they stepped into the wardrobe? She couldn't remember.

"Did you say Mrs Henderson was there, in the basement?" Mish's eyes were glowing with excitement.

"She said that…" Kess scrunched up her face; it was important that she remember the exact words. "Willow Close exists to stop the evil that lives in Willow Hill."

"What does that mean?" Mish waved at Travis again. "Coffee, make coffee." He rolled his eyes at her, but he started looking through the kitchen cupboards.

"Next to the machine, and above the fridge," called Kess.

"What evil lives in Willow Hill?"

"I have no idea." Kess rubbed her eyes. The dream was purging itself from her mind faster than she could hold onto it.

Mish stretched out a hand and stroked her shoulder. "We'll figure this out."

The coffee machine rumbled to life and after a few moments, the smell of coffee started to drift through the apartment. "Milk, sugar?" called Travis.

"Both," called Kess.

"Do you have low fat milk?" asked Mish, without much hope, "or non-dairy creamer?" Kess shook her head. "Just the tiniest bit of milk for me," Mish called.

Kess scratched her head. "You are super slim. Some real milk might be good for you."

Mish stuck out her tongue, then grinned. "Besides, you already fed me all those pizza rolls. When life gets back to normal, I'm going to have to spend days on the elliptical."

Kess shook her head again. "I wouldn't set foot in a gym if you paid me."

Travis appeared from the kitchen holding two steaming mugs of coffee. Milky and sweet for Kess, and dark, almost black for Mish. He set them down and retrieved a mug for himself, with no milk at all. "I keep telling her not to worry, she looks great." Travis stroked Mish's hair as he passed, then he plonked into the armchair.

"How do you stay so average?" Mish looked Kess up and down, "given your diet and apparent lack of exercise?"

"It's more about amounts than what you actually eat," Kess said vaguely with a shrug. "Anyway, who cares. I just do what I want and let my body sort itself out. It's not like it wants to go to the gym either."

Mish looked both exasperated and admiring. Travis chuckled as he drank his coffee. Given the state of his abs, the gym was probably his second home, but he made no comment.

"So, what's the plan?" asked Kess.

"I think we need to talk to David. See what he really knows."

Kess thought about the expression on David's face when he had looked at the photograph. He knew something. She could feel it. Meanwhile, Mish sipped at her coffee, blew on it, sipped it again, then finally put it down on the coffee table.

"Too hot?" That was what happened when you didn't deign to add enough nice cold milk. Kess tried not to look too smug as she drank her own perfectly temperate beverage. Mish rolled her eyes.

"I don't think you should stay here, after what happened last night." Travis had a serious look on his face as he sipped his scalding coffee. The heat didn't seem to bother him at all.

"You said no one was out there."

"I didn't see anyone. That's not the same thing. Mish's place would be safer. The security in her building is ridiculous."

Kess's eyes roamed to the kitties, who were starting to yawn and stretch and give the humans dirty glances for making so much noise so early in the morning. If this place wasn't safe, then they weren't safe either.

Travis followed her gaze. "I know someone who could watch them, just until things are more stable. Her place is practically an animal shelter anyway."

"Her?" Mish arched her eyebrows at Travis.

"My sister," he grinned at her. "She's an animal nut. She'd definitely take them in."

Kess nodded, thinking it over. It was a good idea to make sure Finnegan and Gremlin didn't get caught up in the Family Man situation. Her mind replayed the scene from Mrs Henderson's back yard. The cats posed on the swings. She shuddered. She couldn't even entertain the thought of something terrible happening to her little Gremlin. And big, old Finnegan was such a marshmallow, he didn't deserve any more trauma in his cat life.

Something dinged. Travis pulled a phone from his pocket and checked the screen. He swiped a few things and frowned.

"What is it?" Mish sounded anxious.

"My guy...the one I thought might be able to trace the message. I had a chat with him late last night and sent the details. And it looks like he found it."

"Found what?" Kess sipped at her coffee.

"An address. For whoever sent you that message. 149 Willow Close."

Kess choked on her coffee. Mish slid off the arm of the sofa, toppling onto the floor in a wild tangle of limbs. She righted herself and climbed to her feet, looking flustered. Meanwhile, Kess was still coughing. Coffee was coming out her nose. Travis was shaking his head at both of them.

Mish sat firmly on the sofa and banged Kess on the back. Kess spluttered.

"That's not the orphanage, but it's definitely somewhere in the estate," Mish studied Kess's face. "Does that specific address mean something to you?"

Kess couldn't find her voice. Her head spun and whirled. In her mind, a hand with bleeding knuckles reached out to open a rusty gate. There was the whir of a drill, and somewhere close by, a knife went *snick snick snick.*

9

Mish shifted from foot to foot. "Can we get on with it?"
Kess twisted her face. "I feel like a stalker."

They were hovering on David Collier's front porch, debating whether to press the bell. It was a trim blue house, with red geraniums growing in neat boxes to each side. It seemed like a nice, quiet neighborhood. The front of the house even looked out across the water. It was quite close to Mrs Henderson's place, Kess thought. West Haven comprised a large area, but both David and Mrs Henderson were near the water, in the vicinity of the yacht club.

When they left Kess's place that morning, Travis departed in the direction of the station to talk with his friend. He had taken the kitties, promising to drop them at his sister's house on the way. Kess had packed her laptop and a change of clothes into a backpack and slung it into the trunk of Mish's car. She wasn't planning to go back to her apartment until this was over. As she tossed her backpack, pale pink with pawprints and a kitty-tail decoration, she had a flash. A blue backpack. A transformers' patch. Optimus Prime giving her the thumbs up. She'd paused, staring blankly into space. Mish had put a hand on her shoulder and said everything would be ok. But Kess wondered. Would things be ok, really? She had a niggling feeling in her stomach that refused to go away. A feeling that said things were only going to get worse. Maybe a lot worse.

"If we stand out here too long, someone will probably call the neighborhood watch."

With a deep breath, Kess lunged forward and pressed the bell. Music chimed somewhere inside. Then the sound of footsteps.

They were unsure about cornering David at his house, though they needed to talk to him. The original plan had been to find him at school. But when they had stopped in at the principal's office, they had been swiftly told by Ms Robinson that David was absent today.

"Where is he?" Mish had asked, worried.

"I can't divulge that information." Ms Robinson had said, tetchily. She appeared to have remembered them from their previous visit. Perhaps David had enlightened her about their conversation and revealed their precious angel Timothy for the fictitious ruse he was. Suffice to say, she was unwilling to help.

They had been at a loss, wandering the corridor outside his classroom when quite by accident they had run into one of the kindergarten teachers. The small blonde woman, with blue eyes almost too big for her face, had been standing outside a classroom down the hall from David's, holding two small children, one with each hand.

"I think David called in sick today," she had said when they asked. "Now, Molly, tell Miranda where Mr Stuffles is." This was directed to the small child grasped in her left hand, who was peering up at her with red-rimmed eyes.

"But Ms Anabow, Mr Stuffley is my bwear."

"NO, Mr Stuffley is MY bwear," said the other child, scuffing a foot on the ground.

"Mr Stuffles wants to play with both of you," said the woman firmly. "He loves you both, so if he only gets to play with one of you, Mr Stuffles will be sad. You don't want that, do you?" Both children shook their heads, eyes wide. "How about if you share Mr Stuffles? That will make him very happy."

The first child twisted her mouth. "Ok. Miranda can play with him too."

"Can you show her where you hid him?" The child nodded her head, dramatically. The teacher let go of both children. "Go on then." The two ran off together, and laughter echoed back down the corridor in their wake.

"Sorry," she said, turning to Mish and Kess. "I'm Anabel Clements. I teach kindergarten. Are you friends of David?"

"Yes, we came down from Boston to surprise him. Then realized, we have no idea where he lives." Mish waved her hands theatrically.

"We just assumed he'd be here," added Kess, "since it's a school day."

Anabel pulled out her phone and scrolled. "I shouldn't do this. But I happen to have his home address."

"Oh my gosh, thank you, you're a lifesaver," Mish had gushed.

As they left the school, she had leaned into Kess with a faux conspiratorial whisper "So, why do we think the nice blonde teacher, just down the hall from David's classroom, has his home address?"

Kess sighed. The insinuation was so blatant it required no response. "She seemed nice though."

They had departed the school for David's house, which was only a few streets away. Now they hovered undecided on the porch. Finally, the front door opened, and David peered out at them. "Oh. Hello." He looked surprised, but not unfriendly. "What are you two doing here?"

"Ms Robinson told us you called in sick."

"Bit of a headache, yes. I'm sorry, was I supposed to get a note or something? Are you the school absentee police?" He gave a wry chuckle at his own joke.

"Sorry to bother you at home, but we need to talk," said Mish.

"It's important," added Kess.

"Well. Now it really does sound like I'm in trouble." David pushed his glasses up his nose. "Would you like to come in?"

They followed David into his living room. It was immaculate. Luxurious cream furniture nestled against a colorful red-and-black rug and matching cushions. Tables in dark wood contrasted perfectly with the ornate artwork hanging from the walls.

"This place is beautiful." Mish looked around approvingly. Kess was too overwhelmed to speak. Even though she was accustomed to living in '80s chaos, somehow this seemed like her dream house.

"Coffee?" David disappeared into the kitchen.

They followed and hovered in the doorway, watching. "Can we help?"

"No, not at all. Go and sit." David was prepping a stove-top espresso maker and readying some delicate, expensive looking cups on saucers. The kitchen was as neat as the rest of the house.

Kess followed Mish back to the living room. "This place is so nice."

"Not everyone lives in an homage to a bygone era, subsisting on freezer food."

Kess ignored the slight on her beloved home. Because, even she had to admit, David's home was amazing. How did he have his life so professional and put-together, while she was still basically living like a student? "Are you sure we're related?"

"Yes. Plus, from the photo I'd say he's younger than you."

They were still admiring the house when David returned with a neat tray of coffee and biscotti. "Please," he said, gesturing. They helped themselves and he settled into a chair. "Now, what did you want to talk about?"

"We wanted to know if you remembered anything," started Mish.

"About that night, at Willow Close?" David cut in. "I must admit, I thought it was strange when I woke up on the floor of the basement and you were both gone. When I checked the time, it seemed as though a few hours had passed." He peered at them.

"Sorry to just leave you," Mish said, somewhat chagrined. "I needed to get Kess home. But I did call to check you made it to school the next day."

"Yes, I suspected as much." Kess recalled that Mish had said she phoned the next day and hung up. David must have realized who it was. "I wondered when you would materialize again in person."

"What, exactly, do you remember?" asked Kess, hesitantly.

"I was in the basement, then you both came down the stairs. There was this… wardrobe. We walked towards it, then…nothing. I woke up on the floor." He looked intensely at Kess. "What happened?"

"I don't remember either, but Mish said we were talking. About a deer and a dark place." Kess watched his face closely. There was a flicker of a shadow, then David leaned back in his chair and sighed.

"I think you had better start from the beginning." He removed his glasses and rubbed his nose.

They told him what they knew about Willow Close, Malvan chemicals, and the Family Man. David listened carefully, without interrupting, and when they paused, he ran a hand over his hair. "You really think I was there, in this orphanage, with you and this other boy, Leon?"

Kess nodded. "I think so."

"I have no memory of it."

"Can I ask you something personal?" Kess looked him in the eyes, and he nodded assent. "Were you adopted?"

David looked away, eyes roaming the art on the walls. "Yes. My biological parents died in a car crash."

"A car crash." Kess's mind filled with images from her dream. Water and drowning. "Did the car go into the water?"

"How did you know?" David's eyes came back to hers.

"I think I was there."

"Why would you be?" They eyed each other. Kess tugged on her hair, wrapping blue strands around her fingers.

Mish put a hand on Kess's arm. "We think Kess is your sister."

Mish's phone beeped. She checked it, then hopped up. "It's Travis." She walked out of the room to answer it. They could hear her talking in the hallway.

David looked at Kess. "My sister?"

"Apparently. She did a DNA test." Kess wound her hair tight around her fingers. When she had no more fingers to spare, she met David's eyes. "How do you feel about that?"

To her surprise, he smiled. "I always wanted a sister. Actually, it's more than that. I always felt like I *should* have one. For what it's worth, I think it might be true. I would be happy if it were true."

Kess bit her lip. "Me too." When she looked at David, the familiarity was there. Some part of her knew him, even if the memories had been washed away. Initially, it had made her suspicious. But now, she knew she had misread the gut instinct. The feeling wasn't warning her about David, it was reminding her that she'd lost him. "I think I'd like to have a brother."

Mish came back into the room with a worried look on her face.

"What is it?"

"Travis went to the station and talked to some of his friends. They've agreed to go check out the house."

"149 Willow Close?" Kess shivered.

Mish nodded. "He said to stay here. Or actually, more specifically, he said to go check out the ladies at the yacht club." She looked as though she disagreed.

"That sounds reasonable." Kess said tentatively.

"I suppose." Mish tapped her fingernails on her leg.

"What is it?"

Mish walked over and leaned on the side of Kess's chair. "When he told us the address, it meant something to you. What do you remember?"

Kess took a deep breath. "Nothing really. Just a hand reaching out to open a rusty gate."

"What does that mean?"

"It's what I see when I think of that address."

"You've been there before?"

"I don't know."

Mish stood up again and started pacing. "I went there weeks ago, as part of my investigation." She pulled out her phone and scrolled. "Here." She held the phone out sideways in front of Kess's face.

On the screen was a picture of a dilapidated, white-washed house with a rusty gate. A surge of recognition flooded through her and she gasped involuntarily. She had seen that house, over and over, in her dreams.

"You do know it."

Kess pushed the phone away and stood up. "I think I need to see for myself."

"Wait a minute," chimed in David, who had been sitting quietly and watching. "Didn't you say that you think that's where this killer, this Family Man, might be living?" He looked stricken. "I really think you should listen to your friend."

Mish and Kess looked at each other.

David stood up. "You're not going to listen, are you?"

They shook their heads in unison.

"Then I guess I'm coming with you."

He stood up and began to clear dishes neatly away, then he noticed the anxious looks on his guest's faces and stopped. "Let me just get my jacket. How did you get my home address, by the way?"

David opened a cupboard near the front door and rummaged for a coat. Did his house seriously have a cloak room?

"From this teacher, Ms Anabel." Mish raised an eyebrow at him. "She seemed nice?"

"Oh, she's lovely," he said, then added quickly, "Just a friend though," as Mish's eyebrows threatened to raise right off her face.

The three exited David's house and piled into Mish's car. Kess in the passenger seat, David in the back. Mish set the sat-nav, pulled the car out into traffic, and headed for Willow Close.

"This is a very nice car." David was looking around the interior of the sleek SUV with interest.

"What do you drive?" asked Mish, conversationally, flicking her eyes to meet his in the rear-view mirror as the car hummed along.

"BMW. The new convertible."

Kess rolled her eyes and stared out the window. Why did everyone have more money than she did? They seemed so much better at being adults, somehow. As the scenery flashed past, she wondered what she would do with more money. It would be nice to live a grown-up lifestyle, like David and his nice house. Why had she not made more effort to save, to try to buy a place? On reflection, she had always felt something was holding her back. Like part of herself was perpetually stuck. She was treading water rather than moving forward. If she survived this whole ordeal, perhaps she would make more effort. Try to buy her own place. Really settle down. Even if she had more money, she'd never give up the pizza rolls, though. Kess smiled to herself. Some things were just too much a part of who she was.

10

The house at 149 Willow Close looked just as she remembered. White-washed and ragged, sagging on its small plot. Weeds were over-growing the garden, and the grass was patchy and unkempt. It looked like it hadn't been lived in for years.

They had parked the car a few houses down, but they had a clear view of the front of the house and its rusty gate.

"What now?" David sounded jumpy. He had made conversation on the drive, but had been getting more anxious the closer they got to their destination. He seemed convinced they were all going to get murdered. Given where they were, it was a distinct possibility.

"Do you remember anything more, now we're actually here?" Mish asked Kess.

Kess stared at the house. In her mind she could feel a hand with bloody knuckles, reaching out, opening the gate. Walking to the door. The emptiness. The quiet.

Kess put her hands to her mouth. "Oh my god."

"What is it?" Mish said breathlessly, "What do you remember?"

Kess took a breath. "They died. They…killed themselves."

"Who did?"

"My parents. How could I forget something like that?" The horror of the memories, of that terrible day, sucked her breath away and the last part came out in a bare whisper.

David leaned forward between the seats. "Kess, our parents died in a car crash."

"No. I remember being here, in this house."

Mish turned and put a hand on her arm. "This is important. How did they die, do you remember?"

Kess scrunched up her face, trying to pull the images together, to make sense of her scattered memories. "Mom…cut herself with a knife, and Dad…with a drill." Her eyes opened wide. "The same way the Family Man kills his victims."

There was a sharp tap on the window. Everyone in the car screamed.

Travis' face appeared beside Mish. She wound down the window and glared at him. "You scared us half to death."

Travis leaned in. "You don't get to be mad at me. I'm mad at you! What are you doing here?"

Mish gave him a sheepish look. "I know you said to stay home, but we had to come and see."

"You had to come and see…the house of a serial killer?"

"Yes."

Travis sighed. "Stay here, in the car. Lock the doors. I will come let you know what we find."

"Fine." Mish gave him a mock-salute. "Good luck." Travis leaned in the window and kissed her cheek. She pushed him away, pretending to be mad, but she was smiling.

He waited as Mish rolled the window back up and locked the car doors. Then he sauntered away, back behind their car. She turned to watch him go. Behind them, several cars were parked. Unmarked police were organizing, pulling out weapons and putting on protective gear. They hadn't even noticed.

"We're not very good detectives, are we? We didn't notice half the police force turn up." David's voice was droll. But he looked a whole lot happier, now that backup had arrived.

After a few minutes of organization, several police officers wearing Kevlar crept past their car. Travis was among them. When they reached 149 Willow Close, three officers snuck down the side of the neighboring property, and two went through the front gate. Travis lingered behind, and gave their car a subtle glare and an "I'm watching you" gesture with his hand. Then he too, went through the rusty gate.

All was quiet. The street named Willow Close seemed to be part of an old housing development. The houses looked like they were built in the '70s and '80s, probably for low- to middle-income families.

"How can I remember, if this isn't even my home?" Kess scratched at her hair.

"I don't know," said Mish slowly, "but a family did die here, the way you described."

"This was part of your investigation? The chemical spill?"

"Yes. The boy who survived. This was his home."

"Leon?"

"Yes. His name was Leon." Mish stared towards the house. So, Mish had already known the name Leon when Kess remembered the boy from her dream. If she already knew his identity, why had she needed Kess and David? Was she hoping to find more information? What, exactly, was she looking for? This whole investigation, it seemed, was personal. Like she was trying to piece together a bigger mystery.

"What is it about Leon, about the Family Man, that has you so interested?" Kess stared at Mish until she turned her gaze from the house. They eyed each other. Mish swallowed.

In a small, tight voice she said: "David is your brother, Kess. And I think that Leon, is mine."

Before anyone could process that revelation, something slammed against the car window. Everyone jumped and stared. A bloody hand was pressed against the passenger window. Slowly, the hand slumped away, sliding down the window towards the ground, leaving a trail of blood smeared on the glass. Kess wound down her window and peered out. "It's one of the officers. He's hurt."

Mish unlocked the car, and the three tumbled out. The officer was lying beside the car, blood spattered across the pavement and road. There was a knife embedded in his chest. A hunting knife with a dark handle. The man's eyes were fixed and unseeing. Mish grabbed Kess's arm. "What do we do?"

David checked the officer's pulse. "He's dead."

"Was he trying to get back to his car? Call for backup?"

Mish's nails dug into Kess's arm. "What about Travis?"

She let go of Kess and took a frantic step towards the house, but Kess pulled her back. "We need to call the police! Ask them to send more officers!"

"By the time they turn up it might be too late!" Mish pulled against her. "Do what you like, I'm going." She shook free of Kess and charged towards the house.

"We have to stop her!" David took off after Mish. Kess hesitated, then followed. They had no weapons. No plan. This was a bad idea.

Mish swung open the rusty gate, and headed into the front yard. David and Kess followed. There was no sign of the police officers or Travis. Everything was relatively quiet. The sound of a lawn mower rumbled from a few houses down. The twitter of birds echoed above. Children were playing somewhere, perhaps at a local park. Normal suburban life. The windows of the house had the curtains drawn. There was no way to see inside.

The front door was cracked open. Mish crept towards the porch. Kess looked down at the patchy grass. Here and there were spots of blood. The officer must have run this way, out of the front door. Whatever had stabbed him was in the house.

"Mish," she whispered. "We can't go in there."

"Watch me." Mish carefully pulled the door open, and edged into the house.

Kess looked at David. He shrugged. "We have to."

Carefully, they edged through the front door of 149 Willow Close.

The scene that met them inside the house was one of chaos. The three of them clustered together in the foyer, staring. There were puddles of blood on the floor and streaks of blood smeared on the walls. Furniture was overturned, paintings hung askew. The old television set in the corner had been smashed. Papers were strewn about. It looked as though a huge fight had taken place. But where was everyone?

"We have to get out of here," Kess whispered. She had a twisting feeling in her stomach. It had been growing ever since they pulled up outside this house. Now it was like a demon had woken inside, screaming at her to leave this place. To run and never look back.

"Not without Travis." Mish tiptoed around the living room and picked up a fallen curtain rod. Brandishing it as a weapon, she headed down the hall. She peered into the first bedroom, eyes sweeping the room, and shook her head. She continued down the hall. Kess's heart was in her mouth. This was wildly unsafe. There was a killer somewhere in this house. And where were the police?

When Mish reached the next room, the bathroom, she peered through the door, gasped, and rushed in. There was a loud clatter as the curtain rod hit the tiles. A clatter that everyone in the house, wherever they might be, would definitely have heard. With a glance at each other, David and Kess sped down the hall and into the bathroom.

Kess faltered at the doorway. Behind her, she heard David ask, "What's wrong?" But his voice seemed distant and far away. She felt as though she were floating, drowning. There was a pool of blood on the bathroom tiles. A figure lay against the tub, tight brown curls bobbing as she cut herself. Mother. The knife went back and forth. *Snick snick snick.* There was blood. So much blood.

Something grabbed Kess. Shook her. Pushed her into the room towards Mother. "No!" She struggled, desperately. Did not want to see. The whole room swayed under her. She felt like she was falling, gasping. She closed her eyes.

Someone was shaking her shoulders. "Kess!"

Kess blinked her eyes open. The room had changed. Where Mother had been, she could see Mish crouching over a man in dark clothes.

Travis. He was moving. He was still alive. But his eyes were closed and there was a lot of blood. David was holding Kess by the shoulders, and keeping an eye on the hallway. Kess shook free and crossed the floor to where Mish crouched over Travis. She was trying to wake him.

Kess kneeled on the tiles, on Travis' other side, and leaned forward, assessing. Her head was still spinning, like it didn't want to stay in this room. The feeling in her gut was still screaming at her to run. She forced herself to breathe. The smell of blood was strong and metallic in the closed space. Travis had knife wounds through his Kevlar. He was bleeding badly in several places. His eyes fluttered open and focussed on Mish. He grabbed her hand. "Get out of here, run!"

"Not without you." She turned to Kess. "Help me?"

One on each side, they managed to get Travis onto his feet. He swayed, but stayed upright. There was an alarming amount of blood. But Travis was strong. Surely, he would survive. If they could get him out of the house.

"Who did this?" Mish whispered, as they half dragged him across the room.

"He's here," said Travis. "The Family Man."

David took Kess's half of Travis, shouldering him through the door with Mish. They staggered into the corridor, then stopped dead. Kess pushed through after them. "Keep moving." But they didn't budge. When she had a clear view, her heart stopped in her chest. Standing at the end of the hall, at the entrance to the kitchen, was the man in the hood. The Family Man. The hunter.

"Go. Get him out." Kess pushed Travis and Mish towards the front door, keeping an eye on the hunter.

"We're not leaving you." David hesitated, but she pushed him too.

"Go. I'll be alright." She backed towards the front door; eyes fixed on the hunter. Mish and David hauled Travis across the floor and maneuvered him out the front door. She heard them dragging him across the yard.

The hunter was as she remembered from patches of dream and memory. Thick limbs and muscles. His shirt had been torn away. She could see the growths erupting through the skin, the sharp spines that lined his arms and back. Veins and tendons shifted and pulsed beneath the skin, as though dark things were growing inside, pushing and fighting to escape. What was he? More than a man. Some kind of monster. All she knew was that he could run faster than her. He had always been faster. He could snap her neck in a heartbeat. As she watched, he put his head to one side, evaluating.

His eyes were yellow-green, the eyes of an animal. A predator. A clouded substance, like a nictitating membrane, covered half of each translucent orb. The eyes blinked slowly, deliberately. There was something there, a gleam of recognition. He knew her. A shiver ripped all the way down her spine. She felt glued in place by those gleaming eyes.

Something lunged at the side of the hunter. A police officer. She hurtled from the side of the kitchen, barreling into the hunter with her full body weight, tackling him to the ground. Pinning him under her, she pointed her gun in his face. "Freeze." She pressed the gun hard against his forehead.

Kess felt a wave of relief, but it was short lived. Where gun met forehead, flesh swam and bubbled and moved. The officer's face twisted in horror. In that fraction of a second, as she hesitated, the hunter grabbed the gun in a meaty hand and yanked it away. As the officer was pulled off balance, he stuck a knife up through her neck. The blade sliced through her flesh, all the way through, splattering free on the other side in a spray of blood. Her eyes fluttered and fixed open. Her mouth moved, opening and closing like a fish. With the gruesome sound of ripping flesh, the hunter finished the job, slicing the blade through the remaining sinews. The hunter gave her body the smallest shake, and her head toppled from her neck. It bounced with sickening, squishy thuds on the linoleum floor, and came to rest right side up, staring straight at Kess, eyes wide and empty.

Something grabbed her from behind. Arms wrapping around her chest. "I've got you."

Kess screamed in protest, but it was another officer, dragging her out of the house. In a moment they would be at the door and in the yard.

All at once the hunter was on his feet and charging down the corridor. The officer pushed Kess behind him and drew his gun. He stepped forward, firing. He got at least four shots away before the hunter reached him. Hitting him at speed, the hunter ripped through the man. In a blaze of slavering teeth and claws, knives of flashing steel and razer-sharp spines, the officer was eviscerated. He simply ceased to be, dissolving in a mass of blood and flesh. Body parts were strewn across the hall. Blood sprayed the walls and splattered right across Kess's horrified face.

She threw herself backwards, out of the front door, and slammed the door closed. She hurled herself across the small yard, vaulting the gate. Once on the street, she ran for the car as fast as her screaming legs would manage. In a matter of seconds, she reached David and Mish, who were pushing Travis into the car. Only then did she wonder what she was planning to do. None of them could fight the hunter. He would kill them all. She staggered to a stop and looked back. Breaths burst from her in short gasps.

There was nothing behind her. Just an empty street.

11

The air inside *Cinnamon & Salt* was warm and comforting. The scent of roasted coffee and spice soothed their frayed nerves.

"Although caffeine may not be the best idea, all things considered." David sipped at his decaf latte.

"It helps me think." Kess took a long sip of foamy cream, cinnamon sugar, and rich, hot coffee.

Mish was still at the hospital. Travis had been in surgery for hours. It had been a tense ride in Mish's car, driving as fast as was safe across town to the emergency department. There was blood all over the car. But they hadn't dared wait for an ambulance at Willow Close. Kess had phoned the police on the way, explaining what had happened, and what they had seen. After leaving Travis in the care of the emergency department triage, they had gone briefly to Mish's house to get cleaned up and change clothes. The place was an eye-opener. A huge apartment with sweeping views across the city, access via elevator from an equally huge marble foyer, and round-the-clock security. Then they had rushed back to the hospital, where they'd given preliminary statements.

David and Kess had left Mish in the waiting room. Kess had refused to go home, and had instead headed to the café. It seemed safer, and more comforting somehow, to be around people. The police would no doubt want additional statements, there would surely be a lot more questions. But for now, they could close their eyes and sip coffee and rest. They were safe, in the center of town, among people who had no idea of the horrors they had witnessed inside that house.

Kess became aware of someone hovering, and opened her eyes. The waitress, Kelly, was watching. When Kess looked at her she grinned. "I read your stuff, AO3… It was really good."

Kess wrestled her brain, trying to remember what Kelly was talking about. Her fan fiction: she had mentioned it the afternoon she had first met Mish. It felt like so long ago, and yet it was only a few days.

"I'm glad you liked it," Kess said politely. "How about you, do you write?"

Kelly laughed, a bright tinkle of sound that matched her cheery personality. "No, not me. I just like to read. Something that isn't textbooks, I mean."

"You're studying?" Kess wasn't surprised. This was a university town, with students everywhere. Those without rich parents had to find whatever jobs they could to pay their way.

"Pre-med. A lot of late nights memorizing, that's for sure."

David placed his latte glass carefully on the table. "You look so young."

Kelly flicked her blonde-dyed hair. "Everyone says that, but I'm twenty."

Kess smiled. To her and David, twenty was still pretty young. "I started studying around your age." She remembered how she had taken classes while working odd jobs, just like Kelly. "IT, though. Medicine always sounded like a nightmare."

"I mean, yeah. That's why I read fan-fic." Kelly leaned over their table and dabbed at it with a cloth. "Boss is watching," she said. Her nose ring gleamed in the light. "I was wondering, but since you just said you did IT... I think I also found your game on Discord."

Kess took a long sip of coffee. "Oh?"

"*Save the Fawn*?"

Kess's stomach flipped over. The hairs on the back of her neck prickled. "Yeah, that's mine."

Kelly gave the table another half-hearted wipe. "It was great. So cute."

"Thanks."

David was looking at her, probably wondering what they were talking about or why she wasn't being more enthusiastic about the praise. She rearranged her face into a warm smile. "Thanks for playing."

"Let me know if you have anything else. I'm totally turning into your fan." Kelly gave her a wink and sauntered away from the table.

"What was that about?" David leaned forward over the table, so Kess had to look at him. She twirled a strand of blue hair around her fingers.

"I write some fan fiction, and I also write games. Text games. I released one a few days back. Around when all this started."

"The game where the message was left?"

"Yep. The hunter left the message as a review. It was a warning"

"The hunter?"

"I mean, the Family Man." Kess whispered the name, looking around to make sure no one had overheard.

"Why do you call him the hunter?" David whispered back.

"Long story."

David took off his glasses and rubbed his nose. "The dreams. You have them too."

Kess's stomach pinched. "The dark place. You've seen it?"

David nodded. His face was pale. Kess tipped the rest of her coffee down her throat in one go. The sugar and caffeine flooded through her system. But it didn't make things better. David had seen the dark place. She had suspected as much. Now she knew for sure. They were all connected. She and David and the hunter. The deer and the dark place.

"What about the house?" she asked, "Do you have dreams about that? The deaths there?"

"No," said David firmly. "I've never seen that house, or had dreams about the things you described."

Kess ran a hand through her hair. "What is going on?"

"Where did you grow up? What do you remember about your childhood?"

"I was in Boston. I moved around a lot at first, family to family. But then I landed with this big foster family around the start of high school. I don't have memories from before then. I only know what I was told. Which was that after my parents died, I got put in care. No one ever said how it happened. But I had dreams of that house at Willow Close. So, I always assumed something bad happened there, but it was too fragmented before to figure out what."

"Are you sure those are your memories. Could they belong to someone else?"

Kess thought again of the hand with bloody knuckles reaching out to open the gate. She held the image in her mind, really scrutinized it. It had always been so horrifying that she pushed the memories away whenever they surfaced. But when she stopped and really thought about it, looked hard...the hand did not seem exactly like her hands. Something was off. The hand was bigger, rougher. The hand of a boy. How had she never noticed?

Kess blinked herself back to the coffee shop. To David. "I think you might be right."

"What if they're his memories?"

Kess blinked at David. Who was he talking about? Then it hit her and she gasped. "The Family Man. But why?"

David shrugged. "That I do not know."

"How about you. Your family?" Kess leaned on the table, staring forlornly at her empty coffee cup.

To her eternal relief and gratitude, Kelly placed another steaming cup in front of her, and retrieved the empty. "You look like you could use this." Kelly trotted away, to tend to other customers, before Kess could say thank you.

"I think you really do have a fan there," said David, looking at his own empty glass. "But about my family... I was also placed in foster care, and I was told my parents died in a car crash. I can remember the accident, sort of. I remember the water."

"How about me?"

"I do remember someone else in the car. But it's all so hazy. I passed out in the water. They said it was a miracle I survived. No one ever said anything about you."

"I'm assuming we were split up, after the orphanage."

David nodded. "I moved out of foster care at eighteen and went to teachers' college. I've been teaching at West Haven ever since. I don't spend a lot of money. I never married, or had kids. As soon as I could afford it, I put a down payment on the house. I've lived there for more than ten years now. I like the stability."

"About the same amount of time that I've been renting my place."

"Why did you never buy? I'm assuming you didn't have kids either?"

Kess shook her head. "I don't know. I always felt like... It's hard to describe. It was like I shouldn't get too comfortable, I should always be ready to leave. I felt like I didn't deserve to settle down. I never wanted a family or kids or anything, it's not about that. I think I just knew something was out there, waiting for me. I always knew this day would come." She laughed, "Wow, that sounds really melodramatic, when I say it out loud."

"You have a whole bunch of someone else's memories, bottled up in you. And we both have a lot of holes in our past. I'd say it's reasonable, given the circumstances."

Kess drank her coffee and looked at David. "What are we going to do?" Her voice cracked. The weight of the past few days, of her whole life, was crashing down around her. She felt suffocated, trapped underwater. It was all too much. She could barely breathe.

Someone turned up the volume on the television set hanging above the counter. A news report was showing a building near the harbor.

The yacht club at West Haven.

"…don't know how many fatalities as yet, investigations are continuing…"

Kess leaped to her feet and went to stand in front of the television, with David close on her heels. They leaned on the counter together, glued to the television.

Kelly and her manager were staring at the screen too. Kelly looked pale. The manager had his hands on his hips. Kess had never really looked at him before. A stocky, middle-aged man, he was wearing a chef's apron over a plaid shirt and jeans, and had a dish towel slung over his shoulder.

"What happened?" Kess demanded.

"Someone killed a bunch of old ladies. At the yacht club," said the manager. He scratched his stubbled chin. "Real weird."

"Horrible," said Kelly, wringing the dish towel in her hands. "Who would do that?"

"The Family Man?" shrugged the manager. "MO doesn't fit, though."

The television showed bodies covered in white sheets being brought out of the building. Reporters jostled for position as police held them back behind crime tape. There were a lot of flashing lights, police and ambulance, but it didn't look as though any of the victims had survived.

"…comes just after five police officers were killed in a property in Aylesbury…" continued the report, but Kelly had turned the sound back down.

Kess dragged her feet back to their table and slumped into the chair. David sat across from her once more.

"We were supposed to go and speak with them. Instead of going to the house. We could have saved them."

"You don't know that."

But she did. If they had followed Travis' advice, and gone straight to the yacht club, instead of following him to Willow Close, they could have warned them. Maybe those ladies would still be alive.

"If we hadn't gone to the house, Travis would have died," David said, reaching out to put a hand over hers.

Kess nodded, fighting back tears. What he said was reasonable, sensible. They had saved Travis. But at what cost? Her heart ached. The women at the yacht club were the only other people who knew the history of Willow Close. The only people that might have known how to stop the Family Man. That was probably why he had killed them. Now they had no one to ask. No one to go to. They were completely alone. And a group of harmless old ladies were dead. Kess felt tears trickling down her cheeks. What were they going to do now? They couldn't live in the café. Sooner or later, they would have to go back out into the world. When they did, the hunter would come for them. He would not rest until he had killed them. And they had lost their best chance, their only chance, of stopping him.

She thumped her head down on the table. Let the misery wash over her.

"What's happened?" Dimly, she heard Mish's voice. She felt Mish sit down at the table. David explained the news report. Then Mish answered that Travis was finally out of surgery, and that he was going to be fine.

"They said he should make a full recovery." Mish's voice, though shaken by the news of the yacht club, couldn't quite contain its happiness. At least Travis would live. At least their trip to the house hadn't been completely in vain. A life saved, that was something. More than something.

Kess raised her head. Her eyes felt red and sore. "I'm glad he's ok."

Mish reached over to rub her arm, but Kess pulled away. "You lied to us." Anger was bubbling inside, looking for a target. It fixed its gaze on Mish. Kess glared at her.

David half-choked on a sip of the fresh latte Kelly had brought him. Mish arched her eyebrows. "I'm sorry?"

"Back in the car. Outside the house. You said he—Leon, the hunter, the Family Man, whatever you want to call him—you said he was your brother."

"Yes, that's right. You did say that." David put down his glass and stared at Mish.

"I can't help thinking," said Kess, anger boiling in her stomach, "that if you'd been honest from the start, some of this might have been avoided."

Mish held up her hands. "Nothing I know would have changed what's happened."

"Why don't you tell us what you know. All of it. And we'll decide." Kess glowered at her.

Mish looked shaken. She tucked her hair back behind her ears, settled herself in her chair, and cleared her throat. "Alright."

David and Kess leaned forward, expectantly. Mish's eyes flicked between them.

"My deadname is Michael."

Kess gasped as the pieces fell into place. "You're the baby. Baby Mikey?"

Mish waved her to silence. "I was adopted when I was less than a year old. My parents had died, but I never knew how. Or who they were. A few months ago, I started searching. I hadn't looked before, because I love my adoptive parents and didn't want to hurt them. But I got sick at the start of the year, and the doctors asked about my heritage. I didn't know. And it made me curious. Even though I was fine, after that I couldn't shake the curiosity. So, I started investigating. I already had the job at the paper. That was something Daddy set me up with, I think to try to channel some of my energy." Her fingernails were tapping on the counter as she spoke, and she smiled. "I always had too much energy.

"I managed to trace the adoption and dig up the records. I was listed as Michael Hartley, and the address was 149 Willow Close. So, I went to the house. It was deserted. This was back before the Family Man killings started, when he was still up in Portland. Anyway, a neighbor told me about the history. The chemical spill and the deaths. He said he had always wondered about a connection. There were several families that died that same week, and only one known survivor."

"Leon?"

"Yes, I guess they hid the fact that I survived too. For a while, I thought maybe I was Leon, but the timelines didn't match up. Eventually, I worked it out. There were two children who survived that day. Leon and I."

"So, I kept digging and found out that Leon was sent to Willow Close Care Home. By this time, I knew what he looked like. So, when I was investigating at the orphanage and found a photograph of the three of you, I figured you all knew each other."

"And you thought if you traced us, maybe you could trace him."

"Yes. But somewhere along the way, I found out how they died."

"Your parents?"

"No. I already knew that. Remember how I said there were deaths at the orphanage, and that was part of the reason it was closed?"

Kess's head was swimming. "You don't mean...?"

"The deaths at the school were the same style. Slashed wrists and a drill. It was him. Leon."

"That was when you realized Leon was the Family Man?"

"I should never have kept investigating, I shouldn't have dragged you in. I'm sorry," she said to Kess. "I just wanted to know the truth." Mish drummed her fingers nervously on the table.

Kess climbed to her feet. Mish reached out a hand, but Kess shook her off. "I just... I need some time to think. Could you get my bag?"

"Alright." Mish gave her a worried look, then stood and hurried out of the café.

Kess rubbed her eyes. She felt dizzy and sick. It was too much information. There had been so many deaths. She had to blame someone. And right now, even though it was most likely unfair, in her gut she blamed Mish. For keeping secrets. For lying about who she really was. Kess was hurt, and angry. Terrified. Adrift and alone. She had to get out of here, gather her thoughts, calm down and think.

"I don't think she meant to lie. She was just scared," said David quietly.

"We're all scared," said Kess, meeting his eyes. "I just keep thinking if we'd known everything earlier…"

"We couldn't have stopped him. You've seen him. We're no match."

Kess huffed in frustration. "Maybe."

Mish returned with her backpack. Kess grabbed it without making eye contact. "I need some time," she said, scuffing a toe on the floor. "I'll be in touch."

She headed out of the café, but as she reached the door, Mish yelled, "Kess!"

Kess turned and, with some effort, met her eyes. "What?"

"Be careful out there."

"I'm glad Travis is alright," said Kess. Then she turned and left the café.

When she emerged from the café, it was light. They had spent the night there. Kess wandered the streets for a while, unsure where to go. Nowhere felt safe. She couldn't go home. She didn't want to go to Mish's place, or David's. She ended up at a park quite near her house, sitting on a bench looking out over the water. Towards Long Island Sound. The lap of the waves soothed her mind. She closed her eyes and listened to the water, and tried not to think. It was all too much. So many deaths. So much blood. How much of it was on her hands? For reasons she couldn't explain, she felt guilty. Like it was all her fault, somehow. She had failed. To stop the Family Man. To save the fawn. She was a failure. She was angry at Mish, but she was also angry at herself. Though she tried to sooth herself, with the lap of the waves and the smell of the sea, her thoughts whirled round and round in a vicious nightmare. The hunter. The dark place. Willow Close.

Somewhere towards mid-afternoon, her phone buzzed. When she checked, it was David. She watched the call ring off. A few minutes later, it rang again. Sighing, she swiped to answer and put the phone to her ear. "Hello?"

"I know you want to be alone, but this is important."

"Is Mish with you?" Kess couldn't keep the petulant tone from her voice.

"Yes. She would have called, but she thought you wouldn't pick up." That was true, she wouldn't have. Anger was still seething through her. Anger and guilt.

"After you left, we decided to go down to the yacht club and look around."

"Find anything?" Kess was curious in spite of herself.

"Long story short, one of the ladies is still alive. From the bridge club? Apparently, she was home sick when the others were killed, but now no one can find her. She's just… gone."

"What's her name?"

"Mrs Rawlings. Binty Rawlings."

"Did you say Binty?"

"Yes."

"I have to go. I'll call you back." Kess rang off in a hurry and hauled out her laptop. What had Mrs Henderson said? Binty had an Instagram account. Kess hoped the woman had used her real name. In a few moments she had found it. An inoffensive page, with floral arrangements, crochet and knitting. "I knew it," she said to no one in particular. "I knew there was crochet and knitting."

She flicked through the pages, but the most recent post caught her eye. She read it, over and over. *When in trouble, go back to the beginning. Shine a light in the darkness.* Kess knew she was right. Binty was the answer. This was exactly what they needed.

Kess closed her laptop with a deliberate click. She smoothed her hair and straightened her shoulders. It was time. They had to meet him head on. To fight him. It was time to end the killings, to destroy the Family Man. This time she would win. This time, she would save the fawn.

But to do it they would have to go back to the very beginning. Back to Willow Close. Back to the dark place.

12

The huge mansion loomed on the hill. It felt timeless and ancient. A forever place. The blue SUV pulled into the driveway and parked. Kess, Mish and David got out of the car and stood, staring up at the soulless gothic windows, the arches and eaves, the fading brickwork and the solitary attic. Knowing that the evil they had come to face lay not in the house itself, but underneath, in Willow Hill. A sprawling, growing evil that had always been, and perhaps always would be. But as long as there was evil, there were those born to fight it. This was their time to do battle. They walked the path through the barren garden, up the weed-encrusted steps between the pillars, and pushed open the huge, walnut door. As one, the three walked into Willow Close.

Last time they had visited it was night, but this time the light from the setting sun cast beams of light through the dusty windows, giving the interior a strange, ethereal quality like something from another time. They stood in the foyer, on the black and white tiles. All was quiet. There came the rustling of soft fabric, and an elegant woman swept down the stairs. Kess thought of her dream, of Mrs Henderson, but this woman looked different. She was taller, thinner. Slightly gaunt and hollow, but beautifully dressed. She arrived on the ground floor and peered expectantly at their odd little group. "Well now, here at last."

Her grey hair sat straight and flat against her head, with a soft fringe that fell across grey-blue eyes. "My name is Binty Rawlings. I believe you knew my good friend, Dora." The eyes misted in memory.

"We didn't know her well," said Kess. "I wish I had the chance to get to know her better."

"She was a wonderful soul," said Binty, "and my best friend in all this world. But she never really got over what happened here. The deaths. They haunted her."

"The children?"

"Fiona, Felicity and Felix," said Binty.

Kess started. "The cats," she whispered. Those were the names of the children on the noticeboard, the mathematics competition. But also, it was the name of Mrs Henderson's cats. How had she not noticed the connection? But those deaths had happened almost thirty years ago, much longer than the average life of a feline. She frowned.

"I believe the cats you met would have been the third or fourth generation," said Binty with a sad smile. "She's been naming them that way for thirty years. Like I said, she never got over what happened here." Binty reached into her purse and retrieved a wallet. She rummaged in the wallet and produced a picture. The faded newspaper clipping showed three children and an adult man. The man looked strangely familiar. Kess stared at the clipping. The caption read: *Police have released the identities of the deceased as Fiona and Felicity Myers, and Felix Mandel, who were students at the school, and Mr Gabriel Finnegan, their mathematics teacher.* Kess stared at the photo. The man was the one she had seen on Mrs Henderson's mantelpiece. The photo with herself and David on the swings. "Finnegan," she said softly.

"She was in love with him, I think. Never recovered from his death, or that of his students. It was a terrible thing." Binty's voice was cracked with age and immeasurable sadness. "Now, I think really we must get on. Before *he* realizes what we're doing."

"Who?" said Mish, then realized. "Oh."

"Leon. Yes. He will most likely try to stop us."

"What *are* we going to do," asked David softly.

"The answers lie in the basement, dear," said Binty. Kess shivered. Mish took her hand and squeezed. She didn't pull away. David rubbed his nose.

"Do you know what?" said Mish suddenly. Everyone looked at her expectantly. "I really need to pee." She shrugged. "I'm nervous, and we've had a lot of coffee."

Kess scrunched up her face. "To be honest, so do I."

Binty sighed and pointed to the bathrooms. "Be as quick as you can." She walked to stand beside David and put a hand on his arm, shaking her head.

Mish grabbed Kess and towed her towards the toilets. They ran into the ladies', leaving the external door open so that the last of the daylight could trickle through. It was dingy inside nonetheless but seemed perfectly clean. They went into adjoining stalls and closed the doors. Silence filled the space.

When Mish cleared her throat, Kess jumped and almost fell off her seat. "I really don't want to be murdered in here."

"You were the one who needed to go."

"Well, whatever is in the basement, I don't think we should face it with full bladders."

"Agreed."

They peed in the silence, with just the sound of water dripping from the taps. It was eerie and spooky. Cold air crept in under the doors.

"I hope we don't get murdered at all. But just in case, I wanted to say sorry, for being angry and running off. It was a lot to process," Kess sighed.

"I don't blame you. I could have handled things better. But it's been a lot for me too."

"I get that."

Kess readjusted her clothes and could hear Mish doing the same. They flushed and exited cubicles at the same time, the doors creaking unnervingly in the semi-dark.

Mish cleared her throat. "After this is all over, if we survive, that is, can we please stay friends? Even if you tried to kill me with pizza rolls, I've enjoyed knowing you, Kess."

Kess nodded. "Even if you force me to eat vegetables, I promise we will be friends. I'm not going to the gym, though."

"Yeah, I already know I'm losing that one."

They washed their hands in silence, but when Kess looked in the mirror, Mish made eye contact and smiled. Whatever else was happening, she had definitely made a friend. That was something. When she smiled back, Mish gave her a thumbs up. "You can do this, Kess. I believe in you. You're really strong."

"So are you." Kess thought about everything Mish had been through, that they both had been through. The heartache of loss, the search for truth, the feeling that some part of their life was missing. The understanding of each other's struggle passed between them. Tears threatened. Spontaneously, they threw their arms around each other.

"I'm so glad I met you," said Mish, voice wavering.

"Me too."

"Are we really having a moment right in this spooky-ass bathroom?"

Kess released Mish and wiped a few tears away. "Apparently. We'd better get back, or they'll think we got murdered." She sniffed and gave a little laugh. Mish laughed too. The tension of the situation was giving them the giggles.

They emerged from the bathroom and ran back to David and Binty, still laughing. Binty frowned at them. "You took your time."

"We needed a girl chat. But everything's fine." Mish looked at Kess.

Kess nodded and gave Binty a thumbs up. "We're ready."

Binty eyed them. "You are about to undertake something more difficult and dangerous than you ever have. Clear your minds, focus. We must be absolutely prepared. Failure is not an option here. Do you understand?"

Everyone nodded solemnly, laughter forgotten. Butterflies gnawed in Kess's stomach.

In silence, Binty led the way to the metal door behind the stairs. She reached behind it and flicked a switch. Light flooded the stairwell.

"This place has electricity?" The three were floored. Kess was so taken aback she almost started laughing again. With a quick glance, she could tell Mish felt the same. All those moments, tiptoeing around in the dark. All that time, the house had working lights?

"We pay the bills. We are its caretakers and its confidants. We leave the outside as derelict as it is so people don't realize."

That made sense. Willow Close was a lot more functional than it let on. What other secrets were hidden beneath the surface?

"So that homeless person who died here a few weeks ago…"

Binty held up a hand. "That is a very long story, one of competing factions among the witch world, but suffice to say he unleashed it. The thing we had buried here."

"What on earth?" The answer definitely raised more questions than it answered, but Binty was not about to pause and sate their curiosity.

"Come on, children, time is short." Binty ushered them down the stairs, prodding them in the backs with a wizened finger in order to make them move faster.

The basement was as Kess remembered it. Long drapes around the walls, a circle with strange symbols inscribed on the floor, and a huge, foreboding wardrobe at one end. All that was missing was the buffet table, and the teachers gathered with their small plates and glasses. And the punch bowl with its swirling red liquid. Instead, a pile of chains lay broken around the wardrobe. It was as Mish had said, like something had broken free.

"It's only me now," said Binty sadly. "I hope I will be strong enough." She prodded the three of them up the room towards the wardrobe.

"Wait. Mrs Rawlings. What happened down here? What is 'the dark place'?"

Binty sighed. "This is no time for a history lesson."

"We need to know what happened," said David, "if we are going to fight it."

"We need to know what it is," echoed Mish.

"We need to know what to do," said Kess.

Binty removed a jar of pink powder from her purse, and began pouring it onto the white lines marked on the black, marble floor. She took a deep breath.

"A being dwells beneath Willow Hill. A dark, ancient being. The house was built here, for this very reason. For centuries, we have communed with the beast."

"The evil that lives in Willow Hill?

"No," said Binty, sprinkling dust. "The creature is a benevolent being. It feeds on memories, and helps young ones regain their strength. Those troubled souls, we fed their memories to the beast and it healed them. Made them strong again."

"I don't understand."

"That is the secret of the dark place, dear. It is a place where you face your demons and defeat them. It gives you back your life."

"But I never could. I never saved the fawn." Kess wound her hair around her fingers. How could it be true? The dark place wasn't good, it was evil. Wasn't it?

"The creature was corrupted."

"By Leon," said Mish, slowly.

"Yes. We did not know that boy had been exposed to the chemical spill. We only knew his parents had died. Back then, no one had made that link. That the chemicals turned people's minds against them, made them hurt themselves. The oil, you see, it leaked in and changed them. Destroyed their minds." Kess remembered the oil, in the bedroom, running down the wall. Her parents, or rather Leon's parents, touching it, smearing it between their fingers.

"Leon came to us a dark, troubled child, barely able to speak after witnessing his parents' brutal deaths. We put him in the dark place, hoping to help him. Instead, the oil seeped out of Leon and into that place. The creature was tainted. At first, we did not know why it wasn't working. We put you and David into the dark place with him, hoping you could save him. Alas…"

Kess rubbed her head. Over and over, she had tried to save the fawn and failed. The truth was, there was no saving Leon. There never had been. A tear crept down Kess's cheek. She had carried his memories, his pain, for so long. Her heart ached for this boy, who had loved his parents and his baby brother so much. He had just wanted a normal life. Like her.

"When he murdered the students and teacher, we knew we had

failed. Utterly and completely. So, we did the only thing we could. We locked his mind in the dark place."

"And when that man cast incantations here, it set him free?"

"Yes. We had sent Leon to a care home in Portland. He was no threat, unable to move or speak. But when his mind was released, he came back."

"As the Family Man."

"Indeed. So now you know. We created and then unleashed a monster. It was all our fault. And now, it must be undone."

"How?"

"We must lock him in the dark place, once more." Binty put the jar back in her purse and straightened up.

Kess took a breath. "Is there any way to save him? None of this was his fault. He saw his parents die, watched as his family was taken from him. Somehow the dark place turned that inwards, made him kill other families. There must be a way to save the little boy inside him!"

Binty shook her head. "I'm afraid not, dear. Leon is lost."

"But he didn't kill me. At Mrs Henderson's House. At Willow Close. He could have and he didn't. That means something. I think Leon is still in there, somewhere."

"It's too late, dear," Binty said, shaking her head. "The evil must be undone. You must go into the dark place, while I recite the incantations to summon him. You are the key. We bound him to you. You will draw Leon back, into the dark place. You must leave him there and escape. It is the only way."

"Why me?" Kess suddenly wondered. If they were bound together, it explained why she kept seeing his memories. But what was so special about her?

"I know you don't remember, but he doted on you. He liked the way you cared for your brother, David. I think he wanted to be part of your family, somehow. He followed you everywhere. That's why we thought you might be able to help him in the dark place."

"What about me?" David asked.

"This is about Kess. It's only ever been about her. But we always sent the two of you."

"You were the deer," said Kess, heart thumping.

"You tried to save him, over and over, the way you pulled him from that sinking car, when you were children. You are strong, Kess. That's why we chose you. That's why Leon cleaved to you. Maybe he thought you could save his family, too."

It was starting to make a twisted kind of sense. She had always been trying to save David. She had saved him from drowning, when their parents' car crashed. She had tried to save him again in the dark place. But the hunter, Leon, had always killed David in the dark place. Why? Why had she always failed? It hit her, like a bolt of lightning. David was not the deer. He never had been. No wonder she couldn't save him from the dark place.

"It didn't work, because David was the wrong deer," said Kess, thoughtfully.

"What do you mean?" Binty's eyes lit up. "Have you remembered something?"

"Not exactly. I think I just worked it out"

Everyone stared at her. She pushed the thoughts around in her mind. She was right, she had to be. "This is not about me," said Kess, slowly. "This is about Mish."

"I see," said Binty, stroking her chin. "You believe Michelle is the deer. Or perhaps I should say *Michael*. Not to offend, you understand, but because Leon still thinks of you that way, as a baby. He always believed you died that day."

"He blamed himself," said Kess. "Baby Mikey is the fawn. Which means Mish is the one that needs to be saved from the dark place."

"I don't really understand," said Mish, shifting uncomfortably. "I'm a deer?"

"It is time," said Binty ominously. She started chanting a strange string of words that made no sense. The wardrobe started to shake and shudder. Its doors swung open. They could see inside. There was no back on the wardrobe, instead they were looking at a crack in the wall. A crack with light and shadows that moved. As they watched, the crack seemed to widen.

"Go," said Binty, "he's almost here."

"What do you mean, *here?*" David's voice rose an octave.

"I said I would summon him," she said between the dark words.

"I thought that was, like, a metaphor!" squeaked Mish.

"What would be the use of that, dear?" Binty's eyes twinkled. Then she closed her lids and gave the incantation her all. The chant rose and grew, seeming to take on a power and life of its own. It swirled around them. The crack in the wall widened and moved. Things shifted inside, and tentacles slowly crept, feeling their way forth from the darkness.

There was a noise on the stairs. They turned as one. The hunter emerged into the room. He had grown since she'd last seen him. His shirt was in tatters. Spines and strange growths erupted from every part of the exposed flesh. Tendons and veins and fibers moved and shifted under the skin. In each clawed, misshapen hand, he held a hunting knife. The blades gleamed.

Kess grabbed David and Mish by the hands. "Come on." Pulling with all her strength, she towed them towards the wardrobe.

David dug in his heels. "I'm not going in there."

"We have no choice!" yelled Kess, hauling him forward.

"Be careful, dears," echoed Binty's voice, somewhere behind them. "This time the dark place will be real. Don't let it eat you up."

They reached the wardrobe in a tangle of frantic limbs. Kess pushed them in and clambered after them. The tentacles reached out, clamped onto their heads. The little mouths and suckers found their flesh, burrowing down. They felt no pain.

The crack in the wall gasped and then opened wide. Before them lay the dark place. Tumbling, falling, spiraling, they were drawn in, sucked into the void between worlds. Behind them, somewhere behind them, the hunter came charging, and running, and falling. Then they were all in the dark place. Together at last. The hunter and the hunted.

13

Kess was in the dark place again. The forest with tall, twisted trees. Blackened, soot-smoke branches waving softly in the wind. Dark, foreboding whispers creeping among the leaves. It felt different somehow. Everything felt razor sharp, filled with a clarity she did not remember. The dark place had always felt like stepping into a dream. Now it felt all too real.

Something grabbed her hand. She jerked away, then realized it was David. He pushed his glasses onto his nose. "Sorry, where's Mish?"

"I'm here." Mish stumbled out of the trees. "What is this place? Where are we?"

"We're in the dark place," said Kess.

"It feels different," said David, looking around.

"This time it's real," said Kess. "I think maybe the incantation was different. Before, we were still in the wardrobe. Only our minds were here. This time, our bodies are in here too."

"What does that mean?"

Kess swallowed, hard. "It means, if we die in the dark place, we die out there, in reality, too."

"Why would Binty do that?" Mish was glaring all around her, a taut bundle of nerves and energy.

"It must be the only way to stop him."

Sunlight trickled through the trees in the dark place, falling on the clearing where they stood. The dark trees pressed in, but the place had a quiet beauty. It had been a place of magic once. The domain of some benevolent, ancient being. Until humans destroyed it with their chemicals. The dark place was not Leon's fault. It was humanity's mistake. They had to fix it. Not just for Leon, but for this place. For this ancient beast, who had never meant to hurt him, or anyone. The creature who had helped so many lost children find their way home.

Kess joined hands with David and Mish. She knew what she had to do. Leaning forward, she planted a kiss on their foreheads, her two fawns.

A dull thud echoed in the distance. The hunter was awake. There was a crashing, breaking sound. The snapping and smashing of trees, branches, rocks. He was coming for them.

Kess spun slowly, marking her direction. She listened as the forest told her which way to run. Grasping their hands tight, she lunged away into the trees, pulling them with her. This time she would win. This time she would save them. This time, she would save herself.

All at once the trees had knives. She could feel their silver daggers. The black handles, wood or bone? But the whispers on the wind said "Save them." *Save the fawn. Save the fawn. Save the fawn.* Kess ran, her lungs screaming and legs aching. She ran faster than she had ever run.

She raced through the forest, and soon she could feel a bright red light on her eyes. The portal. They were almost there. As she ran, the forest seemed to move and change. Sometimes she was running, with Mish and David running behind her. Sometimes she was carrying a small, weak fawn clutched in her arms, and sometimes she held a baby, mewling and crying.

The fawn struggled against her chest, its heart a hummingbird flutter. The baby squirmed and squealed. Then Mish and David were pulling on her arms, slowing her down as they stumbled to keep up. She pushed forward, scrambling over roots and leaves, running against time, against their foe. Behind them, the crashing noise grew ever closer. The hunter was almost on them.

Kess stumbled from the forest. A portal lay in front of her, angry red and swirling, glimmering with light. The way out. Their way home. For real this time. She gathered her strength to throw the deer towards the light, to watch it bound and soar to freedom this time. This time.

Then something was dragging her backwards. Into the forest. "No!" screamed Kess. Not again. Not this time. But even as she screamed, she was dragged, faster and faster, through the trees, away from the portal. Branches and sticks cut her arms and legs. Something slapped across her face, slicing her skin. Blood was in her eyes. She could barely see.

The movement stopped suddenly. She was dropped abruptly to the ground. There were two more thuds nearby. Then someone gave a yell of terror. Kess wiped her face and opened her eyes to see David, in the grip of the hunter. He was hanging in its mouth. Saliva and blood drooled in strings that dripped to the ground.

She staggered to her feet. "Let him go!"

Mish was standing to one side, shaking. Kess pushed Mish behind her and faced the hunter. If he had been a man or a boy once, he was not now. The growths and spines obscured all his skin. Bulbous mounds of flesh writhed and pulsed out of him, like his insides were alive and angry. Monstrous tusks curved out from his mouth and lethal claws grew from his fingers. The knives were tucked in a tattered belt. He had no need of them anymore.

"Leon." The beast looked at her, and put its head to one side, evaluating. Its yellow eyes blinked. The second membrane stretched opaque tendrils across the eyelids.

"You have to let him go, Leon. I want to help you."

"It's alright," said David quietly. "Take Mish and go."

"I can't leave you. You're my brother, and I only just…" Kess blinked back tears. "I only just met you."

The jaws of the beast began to close. David whimpered as the teeth punctured his skin and drove into his flesh. Blood oozed from his neck. His limbs twitched involuntarily. "Go, Kess." He gasped for breath as the jaws bored down. "You have to save"—his breath wheezed from him—"the fawn." His eyes closed.

"David. No!" Kess lunged across the clearing and threw herself at the hunter. She beat at him with her fists. The hunter took a small step back. David slithered from its mouth. She bent down and grabbed him, dragged him over to Mish. Then she stood in front of them. Behind her she could hear Mish fussing. "Is he alive?"

"Yes. He's alive."

The hunter blinked at Kess. Its yellow eyes stared. Kess held her hands towards the beast.

"Leon. I know you're in there. I want to help you. You know who I am, don't you?"

Leon shivered. His whole body writhed in pain. Pustules erupted along his shoulder blades. He threw back his head and gave a low, guttural howl. Pain and anger.

"Leon. This is your baby sister. Baby Mikey. You remember? The baby didn't die that day. Do you understand? She's still alive!"

The beast shuffled and shook. A row of spines burst from its back, blood and filth spattering the dirt.

"Nothing that happened that day was your fault. Please understand! There was a chemical spill, and it made your parents hurt themselves. But they loved you. And they loved your baby sister. Very much. You have to save her. You have to help me save her. I have to save the fawn."

Kess turned her head, and gestured to Mish. She pulled David to his feet. He swayed, blood leaking from a deep gash across his shoulder and the gruesome set of puncture wounds in his neck, but he seemed alright. He leaned into Mish and she put an arm around him.

"We are going to get out of here. All of us. What do you say?"

The beast shuddered. Something was happening to its body. The pustules were deflating and the spines were retracting. It was listening. It understood her words. Maybe she really could save them all.

A ripple went through the trees. Dark whispers. It felt as though the whole forest blinked.

There was a groan behind her. Kess turned. Mish was backing away from David, her hands to her mouth. A huge blackened tree branch stuck out of his chest. It had gored right through him. Blood gushed from the wound, spilling his life across the damp, forest earth. David was shaking, convulsing. His eyes flickered. His body jerked, a huge spasm shuddered through him, and then his eyes opened and fixed. He didn't move again.

Kess was frozen. Numb. What had just happened?

"Run!" A guttural voice, cracked and broken, came from just behind her. She turned her head to see the hunter. He was shrunken, mishappen. The growths and muscles had deflated and now she could see the boy, Leon, staring back at her. "Run," he said again. "Save the fawn. Save my sister."

The forest rumbled, earth moving and shaking. The trees closed in. The dark place was collapsing. A branch whipped towards them, ripping and twisting and alive. Leon lunged at it, stopping it with the full weight of his body. "Go!" he yelled, fighting and struggling. His feet dug into the dirt.

"Thank you." Kess met his yellow eyes one last time, and then turned and grabbed Mish by the hand. They ran. At times she towed Mish behind her. At times she grasped a tiny, struggling deer to her chest. She pushed through the collapsing forest, faster and faster. Trees and leaves and branches rained around them. Dirt and dust whirled until they could barely see their path. But Kess could do this with her eyes closed. And she did. Scrunching her eyelids shut, she ran. Faster than ever.

They emerged from the forest to find themselves on a precipice. The red portal gleamed above them, tantalizing and just out of reach. The edge of the crevice teetered, giving way to the fury of the forest. Clutching the deer to her chest, Kess leaped. She bounded into the air like a gazelle. Flying, flying, flying. She hurled the deer towards the portal. It sailed with a surprised bleat, higher, higher.

Behind her, the dark place ceased to be. She could feel the empty nothing, grasping for her, yearning to pull her backwards. But in her heart, Kess knew she would make it. This time, she would win.

This time—just this once–she would save the fawn.

Epilogue

The neat, blue house with the pretty red geraniums on the porch and the enviable view of the water, was turning out to be a bigger pain than she had imagined.

"Put your back into it." A voice snarked from under a tower of boxes.

"I am," Kess huffed, indignant.

They carried the boxes into the hallway and dropped them. The top box teetered, and both lunged to restrain it before it fell.

"Careful!"

"Who do you think you're talking to? Careful? I gave up my weekend for this. Travis wanted to go whitewater rafting." Mish hefted the top box back into place with a grunt of effort and gave Kess a grin.

Kess screwed up her face. "Why would anyone want to go whitewater rafting? Just think of this as exercise. It's probably way better than the gym."

"Watch it, or I am going to force feed you so many vegetables."

The pair wiped the sweat from their faces as they dissolved into giggles. Moving house was turning out to be a whole lot of work, but it was worth it. The house was perfect, and being here reminded her of him, her brother. David. Mish had explained how, the morning they went to the yacht club when Kess was down by the harbor, he had wanted to stop in at an office in the city. It turned out he had stopped by his lawyer and changed his will. He knew what they were doing was dangerous, that he might not survive. And his first thought had been of her, the sister he had known his whole life and only just met. He had given her his life. A life she had never believed she deserved. A new start.

Kess's eyes moved to the framed picture sitting in pride of place on the mantelpiece, her and David on the swings with a smiling Mrs Henderson and Mr Finnegan. She had asked the nephew if she could have the photo, and he hadn't objected.

"He would have wanted you to be happy here." Mish knew the look on Kess's face. She had seen it a lot in the past few weeks.

"I barely knew him, but I miss him, you know."

"Of course you do. He was family."

Kess met Mish's eyes and a look passed between them. They had both lost a brother that day. They didn't talk about it much. The wardrobe. The deer and the dark place. Willow Close. The orphanage was still there, maintained under Binty's ever watchful eyes. But the dark place was gone. The rift had closed, taking David and Leon with it. But at least it was over. No more murders. No more Family Man.

"Come here. I made something for you." Mish gestured her towards the kitchen. She retrieved a jug from the fridge, and poured some yellowish liquid into a glass. "Here."

Kess took the glass with a frown and sipped. She choked on a mouthful of acidic lemonade.

Mish grinned. "Binty gave me the recipe."

Kess grinned back. "I've almost missed this stuff. Thanks."

Finnegan emerged from his inspection of the new bedroom and wound around her legs. A small miaow from the sofa meant Gremlin approved of the new seating arrangements. Kess moved between them, giving them head scratches. "I'm glad you kitties like it here."

"You've got your own little family now," Mish said.

"You're a part of that family too, you know. For as long as you want to be."

"You're not getting rid of me ever, after everything we've been through."

"Besties for life." They smiled at each other. "Sisters."

The cats bounded around the living room, chasing each other. "You know, I have two computers. I could totally teach you how to play."

"I dunno." Mish looked skeptical as Kess towed her towards her new gaming setup. Kess plonked a headset over Mish's ears, then sat down and put her own pink headset on.

"Ok, let's play for a couple hours. We deserve a break. And there's plenty of pizza rolls in the freezer if we get hungry."

"Are you serious?"

Kess burst into laughter, and after a moment, Mish joined in. The kitties darted around the room, playing. Just another beautiful day in New Haven. Blue skies and summer sun and nothing to worry about.

Inside an old, deserted mansion, a huge building made of arches and windows that was once an orphanage, there was a basement. Inside the basement, a room of strange symbols and draped curtains, there was a wardrobe. The wardrobe was pushed up hard against the wall. It was a huge, wooden wardrobe with carved figures of angels and demons and mythological creatures. It was scarred and scratched, as if it had been in a war zone, and perhaps it had. It was shaking. Wood shavings slipped and scraped, falling like sawdust.

From behind the wardrobe came a light. A light with shadows that moved. Stretching, reaching, sneaking out, something slithered across the light. A tentacle with little suckers and mouths, opening and closing. At the end of the tentacle was a single eyeball. It was gleaming yellow, with a filmy membrane stretched half across its width. Slowly, languorously, the eyeball blinked. Noises could be heard in the dark. The rustle of trees moving to some unspoken breeze. Scrapes and cries. And whispers, that spoke of a dark place. A very dark place.

www.ingramcontent.com/pod-product-compliance
Lightning Source LLC
Chambersburg PA
CBHW051709180726
48283CB00004B/1272